Cries of support behind me became screams of pain and death. All around was hysteria. It looked like we were to be leveled in no time. Smith was petrified at the sight of Martino and couldn't move. I butted him with my rifle hard enough across the shoulder to startle and move him. I screamed for him to return fire. Grayson was shouting into the radio for help. All I could see were tracers heading right for us. It looked hopeless until Rich's people finally made it across to us. Their fire support was hitting the enemy perfectly on both sides. For a moment their attacks stopped, as if they were totally puzzled and befuddled by the attack coming from the other side. Some of their fire redirected toward Rich. Some back to us. Some had stopped. Their strength was falling somewhat. I yelled for Grayson and Smith to pull back with me towards Johnson and for the rest to give support backing them up.

The Valor of Francesco D'Amini

DOMINIC N. CERTO

MANOR
BOOKS
INC.

To the many wonderful men I served with. Those who lived and died.
To their families, who endured the tortures of waiting and hoping.
And to my children, Dominic Jason and Laurann Marie, two small people, innocent and free of hate.

CONTENTS

Somewhere between two chains of mountains and flat-lands leading to the delta rests a strip of land known as the "Dakota." It is supported by two Marine battalions, an Army division, some advisory units, a naval hospital, and one small Air wing composed mostly of light helicopters and small reconnaissance planes. A small Artillery is set up in Army's division which forces out 106 shellings daily. The strip of land between the flatlands and mountains, slopes into a valley, with thick jungle brush on both sides and a small river or creek rushing through the center. The river is thick with mud and brush that falls from the terrain surrounding it; the ground has been reshaped with the turrets of war and incoming artillery. In the valley, north of the river and just below the mountains and hills lies a small village called "Kiem-Lai" (population about 100, including women and children). The land around it supports only minimal rice development, so the people are poor and suffer from malnutrition. Most of their sustenance comes from passing platoons, supporting armies, and heroes and victors of the most recent battle. In turn, they provide a half-dozen willing women, bartered booze, night lodging, and the latest information on infiltrators to the highest bidder. Some of their sons and daughters have left the village and set up hooches elsewhere in the valley, where ground has more moisture and substance to support life. These small villages grow no larger than ten to twenty in size and find their setting nearest to the river and close to the flatland. Others have left for the cities— Danang, Saigon, Fu-Bai—anywhere north or south of God's forsaken "Dakota."

The Dakota stretches about eight klicks or kilometers, constantly patrolled by two companies of Marines, each on a sweep of the valley from north to south and east to west. Sniper fire is the biggest threat, along with malaria, dysentery, jungle rot, and the ever-present fear of full-scale attack by the North Vietnamese or Cong. The valley's only value is as an entrance to a major corridor leading to a large Air wing, Support Hospital, Strategic Headquarters, and supply of Army, Navy, and Marines. For the past two years, there hasn't been a major battle, but on two occasions, the Marines tried to establish small L.Z.'s or Landing Zones for helicopter deliveries and transport. On both occasions, they were stopped due to constant small attacks and ambushes on construction teams. In the end, H.S. (Headquarters and Supply) decided to give up the plan with the excuse that it wasn't essential and that combat forces could be supported from the surrounding battalions and divisions along the mountains and flatlands. Air transport and supply drop-offs were made with the utmost care. The valley seemed calm most of the time, but the minuté air traffic or delivery was evident, attacks from the ground came out of nowhere often in the form of anti-aircraft, causing helicopter crashes. This limited supply deliveries, reconnaissance surveys, and general refreshing or replacing of combat troops. The valley sweepers were known as "The Walking Dead." They carried a minimum of supplies and quite often cared for and carried their own wounded for many days, before help could be provided. The constant harassment of sniper fire and small ambushes made life miserable, not to mention death.

Each platoon had an operation, frequently repeating a previous performance. Clear a small overlooking hill, survey the valley, locate sniper basings or any Cong activity, send out night killer teams, establish small op's (outposts), call in artillery to pepper congested portions of the valley. It sounded easier than it looked. Many platoons suffered needless casualties for a small piece of unstrategic land.

One platoon, more often than others, encountered the most challenging operations. The men of the First Platoon were young, dedicated, and most of all, crazy. Most of the men were veterans of previous battles and many, of previous wounds. So, although chronologically they epitomized youth, their hearts and minds were scarred with the age of war. Life lost its value, especially when no one cared. The letters came fewer and far between, the supplies scarcely, and only delivered when things became desperate. Friends lost friends, with no trace, at times of the source of the attack. Sleep was always interrupted with radio watches, security watches, night ambushes, and night patrols. At times one prayed softly for death to come painlessly in the night as a reprieve from an existence which became hell. Time was meaningless, except for the turning of the seasons and the approaching of miserable monsoons. E.D.D. (Estimated Date of Departure), was fictitious and out of touch. Clean clothes, soft bed and the soft skin of a warm lover were daydreams never dwelt on. The "Dakota" named after the old Dakota bad lands because of its wild country and killing, had become a way of life or death. It hovered over First Platoon like a vulture over her victims. All they had was each other. All that was left was a grain of hope, their last touch with humanity.

CHAPTER 1

Christmas and 335

December 19.

Dear Diary,

The thought of Christmas approaching fills me with sentiment. The air is still with hate and fear. Each person hopes another day brings us closer to leaving. The wet gray sky harbors a musk that just robs Yuletide of its love and tenderness. My thoughts flash to home and the downtown Christmas decorations—flashing trees, smiling Santas, anxious children, department stores' music echoing to customers that Christmas means giving and buying. There are snowflakes in the window, and pine smells throughout the house. Everybody's waiting for the coming of Christ, peace in the world, love of brother and sister. How real, how far away it is now. How hard it was to understand then. It didn't mean anything to anyone. I've got to go on living and accepting the things that are true now. A cease fire has been called but I can still hear the incoming rockets and mortars in the background, chanting a Christmas song of another life. Praying for strength is futile. I dream only of living to see another day, to write another page.

—F. D'Amini

It was in December that I met Francesco D'Amini. A warm but strong individual who epitomized the youth of war. He was of medium height and build, dark of hair, blue eyes which expressed only love and concern, mixed with a suppressing hate and fear which only surfaced occasionally. His face was drawn, soft but with a strong chin and character. He was all of 19 and showed his age but still had hold on a man's deliberations. He was very often deep in thought, appearing to be in a daydream, smiling or making facial gestures as if in some deep conversation with himself.

Francesco was easy to get along with; he could talk on any subject and listened like a counselor. I often thought he had so much respect for his platoon brothers that not even war could change his most prized values. One night while lying awake wrestling with my own thoughts, I watched him take night radio and security watch. We took the watches in two hour intervals to give everyone a chance to sleep and prepare for the day ahead. Francesco took the entire night watch and allowed everyone to sleep. When I asked him why in the morning, he explained that he really wasn't tired and that two of the night radio watches were men who were having serious stomach problems and had trouble sleeping.

He said they would do the same for him if they could. I just shook my head and repacked some of my gear. It was at that time I learned of his diary and the almost religious way he kept it. It was the only time he seemed at total peace with himself. Each entry was as important as the last and they were almost always made separate and away from everyone else. I asked him many times what he wrote; with a smile he would say, "Nothing really important." So it is with gratitude and astonishment that I have his diary now and it is with deepest love for him that I cherish keeping it and telling his story. In the days and weeks that followed our meeting, time or history could never capture the impossible circumstances that surrounded our lives, but Francesco did as only he could.

December 24.

Dear Diary,

It's Christmas Eve, to many of the men a night no different from any other. It's quieter and although the men have hardened themselves to not caring I can hear the occasional reminiscence of Christmas at home.

One of the men managed a bottle of gin. Supplies were dropped over a week ago, not much mail but extra rations. I hate many of the condensed meat rations, but I love the fruit, peaches, apricots and pineapples. Unfortunately, there wasn't much of those.

Some of the men are fighting over the gin, there

just isn't enough to go around, and you can't horde booze when you've got it. Some of the men have weed and are passing it, but it's a gamble smoking it out here. I don't mind it in the rear but out here it's trouble. Christmas or no Christmas, all they need is an excuse, the Cong that is.

Our cease fire is a joke, with only our side recognizing it because we can't be bothered and we want the rest for Christmas. Doesn't the world know it's Christmas? Christ is born and we fight over land and philosophies like madmen. I guess He was right. Brother will always fight brother to the ends of the earth.

I'm so tired and I miss my family. I wrote Mom this morning and assured her everything was fine. Boy, how I miss her Christmas dinners and the fine table spread, the midnight presents and services, my brothers and my sister Theresa. I can see their faces, I can hear their voices. Their letters bring everything to life so I can keep hoping that I will remember. I hope I never forget. I am a man with a soul, a heart and a mind. No matter how close to animals we are, we are still men. Fate, destiny or our own folly has brought us here. If we must continue to live we must live like men, if we die...well, I pray, like a man.
—F. D'Amini

December 25.

Dear Diary,

Merry Christmas to all and Happy New Year. The men are singing, "JINGLE BELLS, MORTAR

SHELLS, VC IN THE GRASS, TAKE YOUR MERRY CHRISTMAS AND SHOVE IT UP YOUR ASS." So it is Christmas and I find I must celebrate within myself, there's no joy in the air. Last night our supply choppers dropped in some nice hot beer and some extra rations, more condensed meat but no extra fruit.

Mom doesn't write but Theresa does for her. All she can say is, "Pleasa coma home, we pray hard and tella God to watch you." He watches alright, that's not the problem. If he could zoom in a 747 with first class accommodations to get us out of here, then we're talking, but I can't blame Mom, she's been through it herself in Sicily during the supposed "big one." I always wondered why she never said much about it, now I know. I hope she's fine. Mom, I miss you and Dad. Dad's been so strong through all this and in everything he does. He's a strong, good father, too strong sometimes. Everything burns inside him, being a man is foremost, everything. He write occasionally and reports everybody's fine, Mom cries, Mom prays, Mom fasts, we love you, be a good boy!, strong chin and remember you're a man. How can I forget with this sweat?

A cease fire is in existence and the tracer rounds are flying in the valley, those poor suckers. This makes two Christmas away from home, will I ever see one again? Jason is into *Mila 18,* a book by Leon Uris, like I'm into this Diary. We're all escaping. *Damn!!* It's Christmas and it stinks. Maybe if it wasn't always such a big deal. At home we could slide through this, but we're brainwashed. Look at the Cong. They don't care. They don't mind. It's just another day with no magic to speak of. Where is that Christmas spirit? Tomorrow will be easier, because it's over and who cared, but today? I know they care. They must...some had red eyes.

—Franky

Christmas was over. The new year was yet to come. Tet Offensive was just around the corner. Our position was stable. Hill 335 was a piece of dirt piled high enough to overlook north of the valley and south towards the river.

Our losses were high for the opportunity to grace the preserved sanctuary. Two were killed in the original takeover and two were wounded. We continued to suffer losses everyday. Sniper fire was sporadic and brief, often accurate. One day a man was shot through the shoulder while admiring the beauty of the landscape below. His whole neck and shoulders were paralyzed. The pain was great, and it took hours for a medivac to set down, bringing him back to the Regimental dispensary.

Our corpsman was tremendous. He never had much to say, but he was good, the best in the Battalion. Doc Wesson felt for the men, but dealt with catastrophies like a professional. He was a Godsend. Our medical supplies were scarce, and the Battalion needed a good kick in the ass to relieve them of the supplies they horded and wasted.

While on "335" I often read, more than usual. It kept me in touch with others and the way they thought, their lives and their experiences. A favorite book was *Mila 18,* by Leon Uris. The story of condemned and oppressed Jews during pre-war Germany, and their fight for survival. It helped me at times. When struggling alone, one became a martyr. Seeing the struggles of other people and their desperate need to survive gave me strength and hope.

With the turning of Christmas, I believed orders would come having us depart from 335. Our sister platoon had been in the valley sweeping north about half a klick from the village "Kiem-Lai." Patrolling was slow, monotonous and frightening, but it was a change from existing on "335." Rotation of our "OP's" were open season for pot shot VC who constantly harrassed the assigned squads. The OP's were placed on ledges around the hills that helped in observation of the valley. Many times their hits were direct, pinning down frustrated marines who cursed loudly at the nuisance. Everyone wanted a firm stand against Charlie—maneuvered attack or abandoning of the forsaken hill.

Our purpose was to contain, not to antagonize; our strategy seemed useless though, never threatening the enemy or discouraging their activity. Our casualties grew and morale dropped. Some marines became treacherous, stealing rations, starting fights, returning pot shots, and sometimes to innocent Viet-Namese people. Like the time one of the OP's took shots at an old popason from a small hamlet below. He was tending his buffalo and bringing rice home. He was harmless, and moved about not knowing the danger he faced from the men embittered above. Fortunately, he escaped being killed, but probably suffered a coronary when he returned home.

Through all the frustrations, Franky was calm. In fact, his spirits were better than ever. The atmosphere was always light when Franky was around. He changed attitudes and reversed morale, telling jokes and being positive. He'd reverse the whole platoon from a low depression and help them climb back to hopeful, happier spirits. Franky was the needed catalyst to change things. He organized debates, inspired hope and promoted laughs. He was more important than supplies or even mail. A piece of Franky was in all of us, the piece we would lose control of sometimes, the part that prevents wars.

I found it easy to get close to Franky and I found it easy to make him my best friend. At one point friendships seemed impossible, especially close friendships. One made them only to lose them. As time passed, family didn't seem quite as close and loving. Living in total fear with someone and pouring out your heart to have it picked up, strengthens the bond between friends. You learn to love harder and stronger. Giving more, not material things, they came cheap, you gave yourself.

There was the cool inexpressible humor of Franky's. One day our Corpsman ordered that somewhere around the hill a "crewshead" was to be dug. The "six" told Franky to pick a spot. He did alright, on the highest extended point of the hill. When asked why, knowing that each man was totally exposed to sniper or enemy pot shots, his reply was, "When they go to shit...they'll shit!!" And so it was for the next few days we all carried our weapon and a careful eye when it was our turn to unload.

Time passed more slowly than usual. It was as if we would never leave. Then one day our Lieutenant ordered us to start packing. We'd be out in the morning. Our sweep was to take us around the hill and north through the river and toward "Kiem-Lai." Some of the men were excited because they had some fond memories of "Kiem-Lai," and some not too fond. It wasn't a short hop or operation because we had to take all our gear, even some of the things dug in pretty well.

Franky and I gave everything a final once over. Our water rations were not the greatest, even with our last supply dropoff. We had most of it in our mortar casings and we transferred whatever we could to canteens. Some of the extra things we left behind. They got awful heavy humping, especially in that scorching heat along with a back pack and weapons.

Franky carried an M-2 Carbine taken off a dead NUA officer. He said he didn't take it himself—one of the men in the platoon gave it to him because he liked it so much. It was more compact than our 16's and "gungy" looking too. He carried banana clips with it, said it gave him more fire power, allowed more rounds per magazine. Ammunition was tough to get for it. The carbine needed 30 caliber rounds. It never came in supplies and you really couldn't order it, but Franky always conned the ARVN's into trading or picking some up for him. A carton of Salem went a long way. Besides, the ARVN's liked Franky, he understood them. Most of the men felt ARVN's were poor soldiers and couldn't be trusted. I did too, but Franky said no one understood them and that they were just tired of war. That they'd been hit so many times they were numb. Like being hit in the chops so many times you don't feel anymore and you don't care. He said they'd had so many different people ravage their land and carry a banner of war, they'd rather run and live another day. The Chinese, the French, the Americans, after a while one's no different than the next. We always told him that someday that love of gooks would get him in trouble, no matter what side they were from. He always laughed it off.

We were ready to move out. All the gear was packed and the men were psyched. All we needed now was the Second Platoon to relieve us and downward we headed. I could see how clear the sky looked and how moments like this when the killing stopped, the country showed its beauty. The problem was we could never admit it because nothing so warlike and far away from home, should be so beautiful or appreciated.

Thinking about the trip down the hill certainly wasn't pleasant, but for some reason it was a welcome change. The air so still and the sky blue, couldn't be more perfect. Besides, the men needed a change. Staying put so long in one place, especially a hill like 335 made you twitch after a while. The sniper fire was more than we could stand, everything was just coming to a head.

Franky was helping me and a few of the other men load some of the extra gear, particularly the mortars, and it was certain we had plans. But what and where? Lieutenant Rich was our Platoon commander. He had a quiet strong appearance that showed convictions. The fact was he never said much, but always looked confident in everything he did. He was a big man, about 6'3" and broad, with sandy brown hair and piercing brown eyes. He looked like a tackle for Army which helped him even more in commanding the respect of the men. He, too, had been wounded. Once in a fire fight with a handful of North Vietnamese soldiers, he was pinned into an embankment; the only exit was straight out. The patrol was cut off in an ambush and things looked dim for Lt. Rich, but being the all-American he is, and with the blind determination that only the Marine Corps can instill, he charged out like a bull, head down, feet kicking, and guns blazing. The world stood still for Lt. Rich and he might have made it, but the careful aim of a nearby Gook cut his direction when he skimmed his back. Fortunately for Lt. Rich, he made it back to his own platoon body and weathered the wound. The engagement lasted all of about 5 minutes, with the North Vietnamese dropping back after a call in of artillery and air support. One week in DaNang in the support hospital and he was back, determined as ever to lead First Platoon to her glory or epitaph. Lt. Rich, without a doubt, was a man not to be reckoned with. He had the look of understanding, but looks were deceiving because he was stubborn and sometimes cold. Most of the men avoided him, and obeyed commands.

CHAPTER 2

The Long Trip Down

December 29.

Dear Diary,

We're getting to leave 335 and all the men are anxious. Our supplies are packed and we just await our sister platoon to take over any minute.

Everything is calm but I feel chills run down my spine. My thoughts wander and I feel something gripping at my very soul. Our sweep is a normal one. It's not like we've never made it before but for some reason it's different. I wish I could explain it.

I've written Mom and Theresa and I'll leave their mail with second platoon. They should be getting a supply chopper tomorrow. It's sooner than we will. I hope Mom's OK. I miss her so. She prays so hard she makes herself sick. Theresa's a good sister. She writes more than most and cares a lot. "Country" says I'm lucky. I've got good family ties, good people back home. He says that makes it tougher sometimes, gives you too much to think about, too much to worry about. Country is like his name, natural and beautiful. He's from Arkansas. He has no family, both his parents died when he was a baby. I never found out why. His older brother's family raised him. He never talks much about them, says his brother is smart and generous, an engineer for Foster Wheeler but that they're two different people. It was tough growing up; there was never any real family. Today we laughed about the Marine Corps being so "gung ho." At times you have to be a mental midget to carry out some of the ridiculous orders. Country can make it come alive. He's got those soft, wide eyes and curly hair that makes you change emotion so easily. "Alright Ladies, you see that hill?"..."*YES SIR!*"..."You hear that machine gun fire?"..."*YES SIR!*"..."You want Charlie dead?"..."*YES SIR!*"..."You charge that hill?"..."*Fuck you!*" It's like this most of the morning, a couple of the real hardened "grunts" are almost annoyed that we're having so many laughs. Country's easy to get along with, though, and almost everybody likes him. They all knew he was an asset to us. As our number one "point man" or scout he could smell or sense Charlie a hundred yards away. He had a keen hunter's sense and good direction awareness. We needed that in the "bush." We stand eye to eye, so he's no bigger than 5 feet, nine but in the "bush" he's ten feet tall. I just found out his real name is Clarence George Chalmers but under threats of murder, I will have to keep that my secret.

Jason has become a good friend too, one I don't

want to lose. He can't figure me, thinks I'm wrapped up in something so remote. So what. No one wants to get wrapped up in this. We're all different, thank God.

The war gets longer every day. The end doesn't seem near. Everything is wasteful, especially our lives. I don't want to die here. Death is my greatest fear but more frightening is meeting it in this place so far away. I pray it comes somewhere else, anywhere but here. Who will find me? Who will care? Who will remember me?

—F. D'Amini

The point man for second platoon edged his way up our hill. He was as happy to be here as we were to leave. They were tired and hungry. The trip was long and hard as witnessed on their faces. There wasn't much of an exchange of words, just a kind of Hi-By, as second platoon climbed on and we climbed down. The Lieutenant kept it simple, not too much said, not too much done.

It was our turn. Our place was below. Our sweep started that afternoon. Country was "walking point," if he could stay serious for a change. The man was insane but funny and always with a joint. When we had a smoke break he'd be making his own brand. But not today—he knew better. We didn't play games down there and no one questioned it. We all depended on each other; one mistake was expensive for everybody.

It was apparent we had to make time, with Lieutenant Rich following Country and wanting to step up the pace. The trip down was tough but worse when pushing and looking to make time.

"335" was a steep hill and jagged with holes and drop-offs that were unexpected. In some spots the brush got thick, abrasive and sticky. Carrying 70 pounds of gear mostly in the backpack made it rough. We were well spread apart, but one slip and we found ourselves doing a review of the platoon.

I liked holding my position in the middle. Maybe it was insecurity, but I didn't like being on either end.

We came down the back section of the hill. The front just showed too much and left us open for every pot shot in the valley. It was a quiet trip with everybody keeping a watchful eye to the front and behind. Suddenly, our movement slowed down. Reynolds motioned for me to hold position. Everything was quiet. He started to move again, proving it to be clear.

It was amazing how a reverence showed upon each man's face as he approached the unknown, especially when the unknown meant his life.

I saw clearer ahead to where Country was. He was kooky, but good. He didn't miss too much. He was motioning to Lt. Rich.

"Lieutenant Rich, Lieutenant Rich, looks like we've got about 100 yards to flatland. We should come out over there on that trail leading north and around the hill into the valley. Should we take it that way?"

The Lieutenant answered firmly, "Yes, bring 'em down slow and keep your eyes open by that ravine.

Then, keep on going till we get north of the hill. I want us to be moving pretty steady till we hit the river and then some."

Lieutenant Rich made his way back towards us, stopping when he got to me.

"Davenport, just before we hit flatland, I want you to stop movement, since you're bringing up the second half of the platoon and keep your eyes open when you get down there. As soon as you see us get across past the ravine and onto the trail leading north, bring the rest of the men back into formation."

"Lieutenant, do you think there's something wrong? For Christ's sake, we haven't even gotten off the hill yet. I don't think there'd be anything so close to home."

"Davenport...do me a favor...don't think! Just keep your ass down and do what I tell you to."

We were to play it safe and I was to get stuck in front where I hated it. I turned around and saw Franky two men back, he had that "what's happening?" look. I gestured to keep cool. Besides the sniper fire we were receiving, there were more mines and enemy booby traps. Second Platoon had hit a shoebox mine on their way up. Fortunately, only one was hit. They were fairly spaced apart. Some of the flytraps they laid didn't make it the way they wanted them to, but some did. Those were a sad sight to see. Lately, the enemy had been making their way into the valley more and more, with sniper fire activity tripling in the previous three weeks. The Lieutenant was expecting more traps and even more mines. I couldn't blame him. It was an eerie feeling. I had to keep my eyes open and my feet in front of me.

Soon, we started moving again and the front section was approaching flatland. Country moved slow and headed past the ravine. The trail pointed north and around the hill. There wasn't a leaf blowing, everything was still. The Lieutenant passed the gully and brought the rest of the platoon along to the side of the trail. I stopped all of our movement from my position. We reached bottom and I watched to make sure everything was all right.

All of a sudden, I heard the crack-crack of AK 47's. It sounded like no more than two or three weapons coming from the thick brush along the trail. I couldn't see what direction it was heading for, or if anyone was hurt, but I could see everyone was down and motionless. I waved everybody behind me down, and I watched Lt. Rich inch his way up to Country. I could see Country was all right because he was pointing in the direction of where the fire came from. Some of the other men fell back a few yards towards the ravine. It wasn't long before the whole thing stopped and it was quiet again, still no movement, still no life. From what I saw, everyone was fine, with the Lieutenant and Sgt. Johnson falling behind and checking everyone. Soon, the Lt. waved me on and pointed to the other side of the trail, telling me to keep my eyes open. I swallowed my tongue, turned around and saw nine wide-eyed faces staring at me. Franky looked pale, but I signaled for them all to follow me.

When I reached the trail, the Lieutenant made a

pushing gesture for me to move in along the side of the trail through the brush, but to keep my head down. He also had his finger over his mouth, signaling to keep it quiet. I started in through the brush and trees. He waved me farther in until I could just barely see him through the trees. I kept picking up my feet slowly, one by one. They felt like lead. My whole body was numb and that empty feeling way down in the center of my stomach started to pit more and more. Every little sound amplified itself so much that I cringed and shook with each one. I stopped for a moment and turned around, they were all behind me like frightened babes. Franky turned his head and looked everywhere, until finally, he focused on me. He looked terrified until he gave a slight grin, as if to give me courage to keep on going... he did.

The brush got thicker and I knew each step brought me closer to questions I didn't want answered. A ray of sun cut through making jungle and all that was ahead clearer. I could just barely see through the corner of my eye, through the trees, the opening that led to the trail where the rest of the platoon was. I tightened my grip on my 16. I had my finger on the trigger and a round in the chamber. A breeze whispered through the brush and I couldn't be sure what it was. Everything stopped. Suddenly, I heard the crack of a rifle behind me. Instantly I felt the dirt beneath my head and I crawled to turn and see what happened. Everyone was down. Face down.

"JASON! DID YOU SEE IT?" Holocheck yelled.

"No, it's behind you, isn't it?" I answered.

"Yes, but I can't see anything, nobody's moving. It was over by Franky. That looks like him still standing! FRANKY, GET DOWN YOU FOOL!" Holocheck had turned to Franky.

"He's not listening. I've got to see what's happening," I said.

There was no more fire and no movement, either. Crawling past Holocheck and Stevens, I saw their bewilderment. Franky was just ahead and not moving. He froze, gun firm in hand.

"Franky, will you get down, you stu...Oh, God."

It wasn't more than three yards away. The body of a Viet Cong, draped over a bush. His head was blown open in the back. Blood rolled down his chest. He was still twitching like a fish and I heard the gurgle in his throat. Franky stood over him in a total stupor, his face drawn and red, his jaw hung open.

"Franky, you got him, thank God. Did you see anything else? *GET DOWN!*" I shouted.

He only stood there, gaping. I knew what had happened. Stevens and Holocheck came running over.

"D'Amini, you son-of-a-bitch. You blew his brains out. It's a confirm. There should be more. Did you see anything else? D'Amini, what's the matter with you?"

"Leave him alone, Holocheck. Look over there by some of that worn and broken bush."

"Holocheck, cover Stevens while he moves to the Lieutenant. And keep looking around. Franky, are you all right?"

He wasn't going to answer. I had to pull him down next to me.

"Franky, you have to stay down. We don't know what's around. Snap out of it, you had no choice. What the hell did you want? You're lucky he didn't blow your brains out. He was right next to you. Franky, can you hear me?"

All he did was stare and mumble, but I knew he'd be all right. Lt. Rich made his way through the brush by himself. Once a hero, always a hero. Everything was quiet and there didn't seem to be a trace of anything or anyone else. Lt. Rich motioned to the rest of the platoon and stopped at Franky's feet.

"What's going on?" he asked.

"Over there, Lieutenant," I replied.

"Shit, who's the marksman? You, Davenport?"

"No, it was Franky. He came right on top of him. Somehow, the Gook must have missed him. I can't figure it out, he was right there."

"Never mind that. We heard more than one rifle." Rich was still concerned.

"I know, but there's nothing else around. See for yourself. No more gun fire. They could've pinned us down and cut loose a couple of times already, but not so much as a whisper."

"What's the matter with D'Amini?" he asked.

"I guess he's a little shook-up, Lieutenant. He doesn't look too good."

"He'll get over it. He'll have to. STEVENS, GET THE REST OF THE PLATOON OVER HERE

AND DIG UP WHATEVER YOU CAN AROUND HERE! I'm going to check this Gook." He walked over to the dead Viet Cong.

Franky stared at me.

"Jay, I had to, I had to...he...he just stared at me...he was staring and I couldn't believe it till I fired...but he had his weapon...I didn't understand..."

"Davenport!" Rich called.

"Yes, Lieutenant!"

"Come over here!" Rich commanded.

"Franky, hang on a second. I'll be right back." I ran to the Lieutenant. "What's up, Lieutenant?" I asked.

"Here's your answer. Look at this Gook's AK (rifle)." He held the rifle up for me to see.

"It looks jammed. There's a round bent against the chamber!"

"That's right, and D'Amini is a very lucky man, a very lucky man. He was one second from eternity."

CHAPTER 3

Honor, Glory
or Fear?

It wasn't long before the Lieutenant had us back on the move again. Franky was still in a state of shock, not speaking to anyone and looking low. The men went through the usual act after a kill and tried to break him in. Franky wasn't listening and he wasn't feeling any better. He looked at me from time to time with a look of hurt that made you want to relieve him of his sorrow. We were moving at a faster pace with the Lieutenant looking more confident. We were well spread apart to avoid casualties in groups. The trail ahead was clearer. Our position was directly north of "335" and we were headed straight towards the tallest mountain, "Granite Head."

Granite Head overlooked the valley like an omen of evil. Ever present and ever threatening. At the base of the tall mountain rested "Kiem-Lai," a small but old village. Most of the men were in anticipation of getting to the village. Depending on how we made our sweep and how much ground we were to cover presented a question of when we were to reach it. Our direction was generally straight with the "Granite Head" directly in front of us. We had a couple of hundred yards of open trail before us. Then the view was brush again, thicker with slopes, trees and jungle. At that point we would probably circle wide and cover more ground. With 10 klicks in front of us and taking our time, we had a good two days of humping.

The men were still watchful for sniper fire and any movement other than ours. Sometimes a can of worms opens when you find two or three Cong. When there's smoke, there's fire, and with us moving along Granite trail anything could happen. Franky was following me. I wanted to keep an eye on him. He was getting to be like a younger brother. Looking at him you saw the depression. He walked dragging his feet and not caring for anything. The world around him didn't exist. It was ugly like everything else we were facing.

It was times like those, when our minds would wander and the slow walking and heat made it conducive to drifting off. All I could see was my wife, Virginia and my newborn son. It was less than three months ago when I bounced him on my knee. I could hear Ginny's voice. Wanting to know what to expect. She always asked the toughest questions.

"Jay, what will your job be exactly? Is it dangerous?"

"No, I'll probably be in supply position, you know how they protect their supplies."

"But, Jay, when you were in Cuba, you always

said you were glad you weren't in the First Marine Division because they were dug in there and you were 0311 (infantryman)."

"Yea, but that's different now. There's all kinds of positions and they're pretty well reinforced. Don't worry, will you?"

"Jay, I love you so much and Jason, Jr. is so much like you. He's got your smile and everything. Look at him. He's our baby!"

"I know. Since I've been home he's become so much a part of me, I feel like I can't leave him." I looked over to where he slept.

"Then don't, Jay, please. We can go to Canada or something. They're all doing it. It's beautiful there. Let's try."

"Honey, I can't. I'm still too much of an American. No matter how corny it seems. I couldn't hide there very long before I'd go stirry for home. Besides, somehow I guess it was going to happen anyway. I guess there's too many of my friends, family and everyone that would never understand."

"What the hell do you care about? Them, your silly pride, or us? Jay, we love you, we need you, Please don't go. I'm...I'm afraid you won't come back...please...oh, I don't want you to go!" She cried and fell into my arms.

"Now, now come on. What's all this crap about not coming back? You know that's impossible. I'm too cagey and too lucky!" I turned, whispering in her ear.

"But it's different. There your luck can run out!" She said sobbing and pulling back.

"Has my luck ever run out? Well, has it?" I pushed her shoulders back.

"No...but." She was biting her lip.

"Well, it won't run out now, and will you stop crying. Our son is going to develop bad habits from you. How about some dinner...Huh?"

"Oh, Jay, I love you." She held me tight.

I could feel the touch of her cheek on mine and her tears running down my arm. How I wished I could be with her and Jay, Jr. "Oh please, God. Don't let me die here. It's so useless it means nothing to anyone except them and they need me so much. Just like I need them. I'd give anything to be with them again. To know Jay Jr. is growing and I can't see it. Damn! Does this place suck! What a waste of Goddamn time, effort and men."

"Jay!" Reynolds yelled.

"What?" I answered after regaining control.

"The Lieutenant says to push your end over towards the right. We'll be coming up slow, and keep your eyes open!"

"Yea, Yea. When are we digging in?" I asked.

"Later on probably. Up ahead by those rock formations and high grass. We can probably keep a good eye on everything from there."

"Well, hold a spot for me and Franky, too, OK? He looks pretty shook up." I turned to look at him.

"Yea. See you later." Reynolds turned back and started off.

At this point I could see Franky had pushed his way up and behind me and I could see he was looking right at me.

"Franky! We've got to pull our end over more to the right, and come up a little slower. Try and stay spaced a little more...Are you alright?"

"I'm alive if that's what you mean." He looked straight ahead.

"We'll stay alive. At least till we get to that formation of rocks up there. We'll probably dig in and take it easy for awhile. From now on just keep an eye on my motions and we'll clam up, too...OK?" I waited for a reply.

"Yes...just fine." He said softly.

It wasn't long before our short sweep leading into the valley brought us to a small formation of rocks and flatland where we could dig in and keep an eye on things. At least until the Lieutenant rechecked his own strategy. Reynolds had a spot not far from the Lieutenant, where the ground looked clearer and softer, but he was still a good 20 feet from Rich.

"Oh man, I got to sit down, I feel like shit." I was tired.

"You ought to. It must of gotten a little hairy back there with D'Amini?" Reynolds asked.

"Yes, I thought my pants were wet, until the shit hit the fan."

"Where is D'Amini?" he asked.

"He's coming. He's taking a piss over there." I pointed by the bushes.

"Hey Reynolds. Why didn't we bury that Cong or cover him up or something?"

"Are you shitting me. What the hell do you think this is? A war movie? Fuck him. You think they give a shit about us. Besides, we had to get the hell out of that thick brush anyway. That shit's dangerous."

"Yea, but Franky really looked bothered just leaving him there and all." I looked over toward him.

"Listen, D'Amini's alright, but Hell, man, he's got to get used to it. We can't go around holding funerals for everyone of these nips. You see what they did to some of those rangers up north. They looked like egg foo yong. They didn't give a shit, and if they see what some of their dead look like, shit, it's good publicity. If anything, we should of cut him up a little like the "Rocks" (Korean Rock Marines) do. That really scares the shit out of them. Fucks up their hereafter, and all that."

"Quick. Shut up. Here comes Franky." I held my hand up.

"Hey, Franky. Dig in. Want a smoke?" I motioned for him to sit.

"I don't smoke," he said.

"Oh, don't hand me that. I caught you catching a couple of puffs on 335," Reynolds kidded back.

"That was grass, and I don't do it anymore." He was annoyed.

"Well here, try this. It's not grass and it won't get you high. Besides it will take your mind off things." Reynolds held out a cigarette.

"Yea, maybe I will." He took it from the pack.

"Hey Reynolds, how long you think we'll hold up here?" I started the conversation.

"Well, judging from that stretch of trail we got ahead of us, probably the night and then we'll head out early in the morning. We'll need a whole day to cover a good part of that, and if we don't dig in here we probably won't find anyplace half as good as this without travelling another full day. I don't look forward to that trip."

"Hey Reynolds. Did I show you a picture of my family?" I held out my wallet photos.

"Oh, shit, Davenport, who hasn't? Let me see." He took it smiling.

"Nice. Very nice. Now if you're smart, you won't stare at it too long or you'll get homesick." He handed it back.

"Reynolds, you're a sweet person. Did anybody ever tell you that?" I put it back in my pants.

"Yea, my mother and she's dead. Just like we might be someday."

"Man, you keep thinking like that, you just might wind up that way,' I said hopelessly.

"Oh come on, Davenport. Be realistic. We've got no control over our fate, it's destiny. It was just luck back there that D'Amini isn't lying with his brains blown out instead of that Gook."

"Reynolds, come on, cool it." I knew Franky would be bothered.

"Cool it, shit! He knows what we're here for and he better get used to it. You too!" He nodded to Franky.

"Well, it always seems your luck improves with your attitude." I smiled.

"Maybe so, but I've seen plenty of guys with great attitudes try to push their guts back in their stomachs after getting blown away. Tell me about attitudes. You see them screaming and crying..." He was serious and sarcastic.

"OK...Ok...cool it. Franky, where are you going?" He was getting up.

"No place. I just want to get away for awhile. You know. Be by myself."

"Yea, I understand, but don't go too far." He walked away, his head down.

Time just dragged on the rest of the day. Some of the men talked. Some wrote letters. Some read letters. Some stared. Franky was off by himself sitting in front of a big rock a few feet away. He looked lonely, sad, even confused. I wanted to help, but didn't know what to do. He just sat there, occasionally writing in his diary.

December 30.

Dear Diary,

Today I must find myself. Somewhere between the doubts, the excuses, the sympathies, I must salvage what I hope is a man. My whole reason for living is thrust upon me. Is life really so cheap that it can be snuffed out by another man so quick and easily? Does war justify one man's fate being ruled by another one's survival? Am I to spend my life in a question? Oh God, if there is One, what am I? Killing was easy and quick. Are we all still animals fighting to survive in this jungle? Do we belong here? Do they belong here?

I watched him die. It wasn't easy, but I watched. Victim of my judgment. Slain by my hand. He lay there before me. I decided his destiny in one second. His whole being was brought before me, and if he killed before, what will be his judgment now?...and what will be mine? His eyes were staring for that brief moment when he faced the omen of death and it was me! His face. Those eyes. Those seconds he was at my mercy, or I at his.

Now I live and I breathe. I hear and I see. I'm alive, but for how long? When will my time come? Will I be dealt the same hand only to have it called, like him? Will my life be worth so little that men will laugh over me and share my last possessions, spit on me, strip me? Will they bury me or will I rot in the sun to warn the next passing troop? Oh God, I'm scared. Scared of dying, scared of remembering. He was no more than 16 and although armed, he seemed defenseless. Please forgive him, forgive me and give me the strength to face each day. Help me to sleep at night and take away the image of his face from my mind.

The men around me find it amusing, exciting and some are envious. I have a definite confirm, my first. I am part of the war and I am accepted. Some say, "Each confirm is glorious." I've been told to forget. It gets easier and easier. I'll understand. Don't lose sleep.

Momma, you taught me to turn the cheek, Dad to be a man., I'm here now as a man and I'm torn between my soul and my very existence. What it must be like to die. To know the final moment is upon you. To feel your last hold on what is your life, slip from you.

Jesus cried, "My God why have You forsaken Me." The strongest of men. Tonight, I take my fears to sleep and my sorrow to heart. There are no answers within me. Only conscience. There is but another day, tomorrow, and I must live. I feel no courage. Only fear. I have no honor. Only life. There is no glory, only memories.

—F. D'Amini

CHAPTER 4

Night Watch

Night came quickly and with the combination of excitement and humidity the men were tired. The mosquitoes clinging to the high grass were enough to make you miserable and so was the dampness.

In spite of everything, the men found it possible to doze off and prepare for another day. Lieutenant Rich had set four positions of security watch with constant 15 minute radio checks to our sister platoon. It was New Year's Eve and not a trace of partying. Some of the men grumbled earlier about escapades back home and the drinking binges, but tonight there was no booze to be found, or girls, or any libations.

The night was peaceful and quiet. The stars seemed sharp and clear. Looking up, I saw the heavens and I thought to myself how seldom I thought of them at home. I became so entangled amidst the planets and stars that I felt like floating. I had 40 minutes to go before my watch would start and I had no intentions of sleeping. To feel so close or "in-tune" to yourself was something we so often lost. It's the most important part. It's the soul and spirit within the body. Thinking about the possibility of losing my life made me want to know myself a little better, especially the part which I hoped lived on.

The temperature dropped a little and the air got chilly. I had to wrap myself warmer. The men awake on watch were alert, constantly looking in all directions, staring at every bristle or whisper of wind. The sky above almost begged confidence that the night would be tranquil.

Looking over at Franky I could see he wasn't moving. He had to be sleeping or staring off into nothing. The poor kid. This was tough on him. Tough on everyone, but tougher on him. He had a good heart. Ginny would love him. He was like her younger brother, sweet and understanding but with good convictions and an independence for his feelings.

The whole picture was out of place, Franky and killing. Take the valley, so beautiful, but so ugly. My being here, instead of home, working and with my family. What a twist. First drafted, then to the Marines. A year ago if someone would have said to me and the Marines, I would have said, "crazy." Here I am. But Franky? How could you figure the kid enlisting, and in the Marines. He just doesn't seem like your basic grunt, jarhead, Girene. Not Franky. What could have possessed him? Well, I'll have to ask him sometime.

"Davenport?" Manny Valesquez was next to me.

"Yea, Valesquez, time already? I thought I had more time." I spoke plainly.

"Shh! Softer. You do, 5 minutes. I thought I'd get you ready." His finger was to his mouth.

"Thanks. How is everything?" Motioning to his watch.

"Quiet. Too quiet." He looked all around.

"Isn't that good?" I asked.

"Yea, maybe, but it gibbs me de creeps. It's your turn buddy." He shivered.

"Tell me how you felt in the morning. I'm sacking out, OK?"

"Yea, OK." I started to get ready.

"By de way, keep dose eyes open." He turned to me again.

"Don't worry. Those were my very feelings. Pleasant dreams."

"They will be. I'm thinking of my Concita. She's warm and soft and uummm..." He was smiling with his eyes closed.

"Go to sleep, you Spanish hard-on." I hit him on the head.

Crawling past Franky I could see he wasn't sleeping. He was deep in thought and staring off.

"Hey you, Wop! Get some sleep. You'll be dragging in the morning. Franky, do you hear me, you OK?" I looked to see if he was alright.

"Yea, Jay, I'm OK. You want me to stand watch for you?" he said innocently.

"No, you asshole. Get some sleep and quit being so generous. Someone is going to take advantage of you. What the hell do you think you are? Chesty

Puller?"

"No, it's not that. It's just that I'm awake anyway and..." He started to get up.

"Well forget it. Besides it's too much fun. Get to sleep. Talk to you in the morning." I pushed him down.

"Jay..." He just barely called me.

"What?"

"....I'm scared." He looked to me for an answer.

"We all are Franky. We all are. We all just try real hard not to show it. You're a little more honest. Now turn in."

Looking across the top of the grass, everything was still and quiet just like Manny said. It was nice at first but started to give me the creeps. It was as if there were hidden secrets within the rocks, grass and scattered brush. I found myself looking deep into every area surrounding me. At times I would count the blades of grass and rocks along the ground. I help my weapon close and checked my chamber to make sure I was loaded for bear. We were far enough from any thick brush to take sniper fire or night attacks, but not far enough to suit me. I started making SIT REPS (Situation Reports).

"Hotel 2, Hotel 2, this is Hotel 1. SIT REPS, please."

I waited but no answer.

"Hotel 2, Hotel 2, Sit Reps, wake the fuck up, come on." I spoke louder.

I heard the three buzzes on the radio telling me everything was fine and all was clear. Sometimes they were a little lax on the hill. With me, they stayed awake, on time every time. Suddenly the grass behind me brushed, and my heart did a turn around, I had my finger on the trigger and...

"Davenport." I jumped out of my skin. It was Holocheck.

"Holocheck, you jerk off. What do you want?"

"Shh, I just want to take a shit." He was on all fours.

"You would, you asshole. Well hurry up and keep quiet. Take a shit...you almost had me take one." I turned back, sighing relief.

"What the hell you want me to do send up flares?" he said sarcastically.

"No, just don't stuff your face so late. We're trying to save rations anyway. Well hurry up."

"Yea, OK." He began to crawl away.

"....and keep a few feet away, I don't want to be smelling your fragrance all night."

I had to close my eyes a second and breathe deep to regain stability, but things were the same, tranquil but mysterious. My heart was still beating fast and I tried to convince myself this was like any watch I've taken before. My own fears were getting the best of me and if I didn't control them it would be a longer night than expected. Looking over at the other watches, I couldn't tell what they felt. I only knew they were awake and alert and they probably were wondering about me. Occasionally I gestured to whoever was to the right of me, some thirty feet away, just to give reassurance that everything was fine. I couldn't tell who any of them were. It was much too dark even with the open ground.

"Davenport, I'm done." It was Holocheck again.

"Good.. What the hell you want me to do, clap?"

"Well, I'm just telling you. I'm scooting back." He was still on all fours.

"Yea fine. Pleasant dreams."

"You too." He crawled away.

"Ha!" I laughed.

"Pleasant dreams"...I said to myself...Christ, it was 15 to 12. Five minutes to New Year and no party in sight, not even a horn. It's funny how the men hardly spoke of New Year, like it wasn't important. We should just let it pass. Ring out the old and ring in the new, ha! Happy New Year, Ginny, and you too, Jay, Jr. I love you both so, I hope you can hear me. I hope this year brings you happiness.

"Davenport!" It was Franky again.

"Franky, will you be quiet. For Christ sakes. It's like Grand Central Station here. The gooks are gonna be sleeping with us any minute." I definitely was annoyed at this point.

"Jay...Happy New Year." He said sincerely.

"Thanks Franky. Same to you. Now will you get some sleep and leave me alone. I gotta keep my eyes open." Begging to be alone.

"OK, but I'm here if you need me."

"Yea, yea. You'll get your turn. Will you go to bed Florence Nightingale?" I just smiled.

What a guy. With him they had to break the mold. It was an eerie night. New Year's or no New Year's, quiet or no quiet, something smelled. Well, it must have been my imagination. Just a little longer and Andretta could have the aggravation. Tonight I was sawing wood. Thank God for sleep. The only escape that no one could horn in on. The departure from this shit world of ours. Funny how I used to think I could never sleep out here in the middle of nowhere, in Nam. I always pictured myself buggy eyed and palpitating heart. No way now. Gotta get those zzz's.

Tomorrow, I thought. The hump would be long and hard. I could see it in Rich's face. I wondered what he was thinking. I wondered what he was like? He was hard as hell to get close to. Everything was arm's length. Every was KOOL! Man, they didn't break the mold with him. There were enough like him in this man's Marine Corps to go around three times. Cold, tough, determined, and most of all heroic...and something else. I couldn't pinpoint it, but it's hidden deep inside, like a memory you try to hide, but somehow it always shows up on the face, and it bothers you. He was secretive too. Not confidential, but very controlled, with something he kept to himself. I've known men like him back home. Some find them frightening, some interesting, some boring. I was still trying to decide. One thing I did find. He was commanding! You didn't say no to Lieutenant Rich. The man was overpowering in personality and appearance, and our lives were riding with his leadership from now on.

It was just about time for Andretta to be preparing for watch. There was no extra time left. It was his turn for the aggravation. I better get over to him. He was off by a triangular rock, bedding down with his best friend, Budchinsky. Franky's head was up again. He was the only man I knew who could live without sleep.

"D'Amini, will you get the hell to sleep!" This time I meant it.

"I am. It just looks like I'm awake." He kidded back.

"You're going to be sorry in the morning."

"I know, Jay...but I can't sleep...I'm too wrapped up in...I mean I can't sleep." He was still thinking of the dead Cong.

"Will you forget about that. It's over! It wasn't your fault. What the hell do you want? It was him or you. Would you feel better if you were in fairy land? Now roll over and go to sleep!"

"Where you headed...watch over?" He was oblivious.

"Yea, I've got to get Andretta. See ya." I left to find Andretta.

I could see Andretta was about thirty feet away. He was off on his own with Budchinsky. They were close friends and shared the same interests. Both from small midwest towns, the same high school. They even dated the same girls. Andretta was the bigger of the two. He spoke less but had a much stronger appearance with piercing eyes and strong jaw. Budchinsky was more the easygoing comedian type, with softer features and a wide smile. There was no doubt. Where there was Andretta, you'd find Budchinsky. They were probably backing each other on watch, too, one relieving the other.

Everything around them was still. I hated to

break up their sleep.

"Andretta, Andretta, wake up, you're on. It's your turn. Come on, Andretta. We've all gotta do our share. There's a war on you know...Andretta, Andretta, come on." I shook him harder.

A cold chill ran down my spine as I could see the total lack of movement. He was perfectly still, with his face buried to the side. I had to turn him over to see his face. Suddenly I could see his open eyes gaping at me and the blood running across his face, down his neck onto his jacket. Total fear marked his face. My God, he was slashed from ear to ear and down his chest. Oh Dear God!!"

"*BUDCHINSKY, BUDCHINSKY!!*" There was no response.

I pushed him over. He had the same face, covered with blood and dirt and his own saliva. MY GOD. OH MY GOD! My whole body shook. My hands couldn't move and I felt frozen. Their faces both gaping at me and covered in their own blood. My mouth was open but nothing came out. I darted a glance all around me and mumbled a quick prayer. Finally, I called out loud for the Lieutenant and motioned over to the other watch. Lieutenant Rich was up immediately. So was Franky and some others. Our trouble had just begun.

December 31.

Dear Diary,

The year closes. Two more dead. They spoke today of a customized "57" Chevy and back seat love. The car was green and fast. Its leather soft and dark. The hours it consumed were countless. The laughs and thrills it produced were priceless. They looked forward to driving it again. It was being cared for. Why is that all I can see right now?

—D'Amini

CHAPTER 5

Death Valley

"Jesus Christ! Holocheck, Smith, D'Amini. Get your asses moving and check the rest of the platoon. Double the watch and get a radio over here quick! Davenport. Did you see anything. Anything at all?" Lieutenant Rich was excited.

"No Lieutenant. I made my way over here to get Andretta for his watch. I saw he wasn't moving and when I turned him over, well...then getting Budchinsky I saw he was..."

My knees were weak and my body trembled. All Rich did was stare at me. Then he pushed Andretta and Budchinsky's eyes closed.

"Davenport, are you sure you didn't see anything? They look like they were just killed."

"I swear Lieutenant, I looked all around and I didn't see a thing. In fact everything was so quiet it gave me the creeps!" Sergeant Johnson was standing next to us.

"Johnson, I want two squads to circle this whole area and kill anything that moves. Get Ryan and

Robbins to head your killer teams. Gimme that radio. Get Battalion for me." He pulled the radio from Reynolds.

"Lieutenant, everybody's fine. Guliano. Ferrara and Davis are helping on the watch. I think Holocheck has Martino over there by Hill." Smith was out of breath.

"D'Amini, did you see anything?"

"Not a thing Lieutenant, and I swear I was wide awake. I don't know where they could've come from. We didn't even hear Andretta or Budchinsky."

"Lieutenant, I've got Battalion. It's Captain Stevens."

"Little Fox, get Hawk on the box. I got two of my men sliced from ear to ear...I don't care where he is. Get the fucker on the wire. This valley was to have been secured. We haven't even gotten into it yet and the place is crawling with these Cong...yea, yea I'll hang on."

Rich was concerned and excited but with total conviction and control. We were all quiet and nervous. Franky stood next to me and I knew he felt like me. It was written all over his face.

"*Hawk.* This is *Bear,* look we're dug in here right past the ravine, north of 47240SK, and we got two "DOA's" here. They're cut up from ear to ear. Somehow they broke our cover here and got them while they were sleeping. This valley was peppered with air and artillery and I know this place is crawling with them."

"Don't ask me how, I know...I know!"

Major Stevens, our commanding officer, was a cool man and always looked at war strategically and with pen and paper. Lieutenant Rich and him had never been best of friends. They never agreed totally on military strategy.

"Look, Hawk. Your air people said they went all through this valley and there wasn't much here except stragglers, papasons, and a few leftover Cong. Well...they're full of shit because I can smell something already. Hotel 2 didn't have much hassle but Eagle says they're here."

I could see Rich was building up to something, and maybe he knew more than we did. Nevertheless he was right. The valley was inhabited.

"Yea...yea, we'll still move in, but get a chopper out here to get our dead, and I need more people. I want air cover tomorrow. I need them to check out ahead of us. I'm not moving in until they do. OK...over and out."

"Hotel 2, hotel 2, this is Bear, do you read me?" The lieutenant called Second Platoon on 335.

"Yes, Big Bear, this is 2. What's up?"

"Gimme Eagle, Hotel 2, NOW!"

Lieutenant Rich wanted Lieutenant Williams and I could see he was going to handle things.

"Bear, this is Eagle. Are you there?" They replied.

"Yea, I'm here Eagle, I got two 'DOA's' here. They got them in their sleep. Are you alright up there?"

"Yea Bear. It's quiet," they said.

"Well look. Keep your eyes open and keep security tight, OK? And do me a favor. As soon as there's light keep an eye through your scope up there and let me know if you see anything down here or smell anything. You read me?"

"We read you, Bear. Will keep our eyes open, and thanks."

Rich wasn't leaving anything open. We had a powerful scope mounted on our hill just for valley observation, kind of like big binoculars on a stand. You could get a good view of the valley from all directions. Right now we couldn't see much of anything.

"Davenport, you and D'Amini keep your eyes open up there with Guliano and make sure everybody's on their toes. I got to go over some things with the 6 (Sergeant Johnson)."

Franky and I shuffled our way over to Guliano and didn't say a word. Guliano was a little shook up, but who wasn't.

"What's going on back there, Jay?" he asked with a worried look.

"Well, the Lieutenant's pissed and he had Connors and Stevens on the wire. He wants air support tomorrow. He thinks the valley's crawling with Gooks."

"You think so?" Guliano said excitedly.

"Who knows, I don't. You just get the feeling it is. I feel like they're watching us always, especially this early getting hit. He called Williams in Second Platoon. Told him to keep his eyes open for himself and us."

"They got it pretty bad, Andretta and Budchinsky?" Guliano questioned with a disgusted look.

"Man, it's a mess. What they did to them, I don't even want to talk about it. Franky, you alright. You're not saying much." Franky stared in the opposite direction.

"Jay, I don't like this whole thing. It makes me sick, sick to my stomach. I want to get out of here alive, I just want to be home. Those poor guys never even had a chance. They way they died...if I couldn't sleep before I don't know how I will now."

"Look Franky. We gotta hope the Lieutenant looks out for us and I have a feeling he will, but you're right. I don't like the whole thing either. Right now we just keep on our toes."

"Jay, do you think we'll make it out of here alive?" he asked.

I looked away to find the words to help him and myself. We weren't well off.

"Franky, we have to keep thinking that's the only way it's going to be, alive and healthy. Right Guliano?"

"No shit, I'm not losing my ass in this hole." He pointed to the ground and turned back to watch.

"We better shut up and keep looking around."

The night was long and tense with daylight creeping slowly on us. Our killer teams returned with no luck or sign of anything. Andretta and Budchinsky's bodies were covered but lingered with us as the smell of death. Rich was awake like most of us and he was pacing, while staring intently at the sky looking for any air activity. Finally, we heard the sound of choppers in the distance; it was music to our ears. We were in good postion for her to put down but the question was, would she? and could she?

We all looked in every direction, waiting for anti-aircraft fire or any fire, but there was none. They circled over and over again as they evaluated our position. They weren't taking any chances, especially after last night.

Finally, she started to set down as another "Huey" helicopter trailed behind her. Rich was getting what he wanted. As the big bird settled down the grass blew hard from her wind and we had our dead bundled up and ready to be loaded. Her big door opened and we loaded them on. Franky helped drag out some of the supplies and we threw on any mail we had. There was a good feeling seeing the chopper. It was a touch with reality, other people, battalion, supplies and mail sometimes, but there probably wouldn't be too many more ships coming in as we moved deeper in the valley. We were fairly loaded up and soon to be in the thick ahead of us.

Our new replacements weren't too eager and they had that anxious look, like scared rabbits. There were two Americans and four ARVN soldiers. I imagined the stories in battalion, "The Walking Dead" constantly facing death and combat. Well, they weren't totally wrong after all. Rich wasn't exactly excited about new people but somewhat relieved that we got something. It wasn't long before they made it over to our area.

"Hi, this Gary Witt. I'm Tommy Dunne."

"How're you doing?" I shook their hands.

"Alright till we heard we were coming here." He looked all around.

"Well, don't listen to too many stories." I smiled.

"You mean they aren't true?" Looking surprised.

"It depends on what and how many."

"A lot, a whole lot." He was being serious.

"Well, you'll get a chance to find out for yourself. This is Frank D'Amini, Mr. Personality." Franky shook hands and smiled.

"Hi. Hey man, they really had some air support set up to follow us. A 4's. They're supposed to rip up the valley." They pointed to the air. Then the trees.

"Yea, that's what they said last time, and this valley was crawling with Cong, at least the Lieutenant thinks so," Franky answered.

"Yea, you guys got it last night. That must of been hairy."

"It wasn't cool at all. They never had a chance." I shook my head and looked down.

"Wow man, that's some scene. I'm sorry." He had a sympathetic look.

"Yes...Hey, I can spot those A 4's, they're coming up fast. Looks like three or four of them."

They darted at spectacular speed above us, then circled around cutting their speed and leveling off somewhat. They glided over us again and headed straight for the valley. It was like watching the Blue Angels in entertainment. All eyes were upon them. Rich looked intently as if directing them to their target. Suddenly, we saw their rockets rip through the brush ahead of us cutting through it like a knife, then over and over again. They probably spotted some activity just west of our trail and they poured heavy gunfire and rockets over and over again till they covered the whole area. It was exciting to watch. Then back over again to where they started and in through the valley with a barrage of constant rockets and gunfire. There was very little anti-aircraft fire, and if there was, it was hard to tell anyway. They moved so fast and covered so much area the whole valley was full of smoke and ringing with rocket and gunfire attacks. They were fast and graceful but you could see they were studying the valley like a cat on its prey. They flew in low and riddled the trees and even some of the open land as if they knew they were even hiding in the grass. Occasionally we heard the moans of screaming voices of whatever remained, but then we had to question whether it was the jet engines, gun attacks or speed sounds and shocks. If there was anything roaming around, I don't think it was healthy enough to roam anymore. We'd never know though, the Viet-Cong had a peculiar way of caring for their dead and carrying them or hiding them. They almost never left them behind. The valley could claim a thousand lives and we'd never find them. We had a tough time finding them when they were alive, too.

With the final barrage of fire and assault, they turned around and flew upside down, spinning over and over again as they continued out gracefully, leaving the valley and giving us their "Victory Salute." We cheered, knowing the valley was a safer place and in appreciation of a spectacular show. The spirit of confidence and strength had returned, with new supplies, some new faces and battalion support. Fear rang through the valley; a new ball-game was to begin.

CHAPTER 6

"Just A Roll
Of The Dice"

January 1.

Dear Diary,

All my thoughts are jumbled. My mind refuses to rest and my soul haunts me; it remains at my side, it controls my conscience. The night only brings more darkness and fear. It is at night I fear the most. Death can come swiftly like the first breath of life and what then. What comes next? A breath of new life or a curse of a new death, or nothing? Might there be nothing after death? Then why do we rob that which is most precious to us now. Who has the right? Are we the masters of our own fate or are we puppets, chess pieces, supernatural entertainment, or just spirits searching for...what? If I must judge another man, I must be his executioner also. It seems so simple.

Last night I said farewell to two more friends, or I should say comrades in the cause, two fellow humans. Their sleep was a bitter one covered in blood and fear. Their night was complete darkness. Their spirits depart. To where? To what? I'm crying for an answer and no one hears. Where are you Andretta? Where are you Budchinsky? Do you know the answer now? Do you see us? Are we right? Are we wrong? Are you laughing or crying? Or ARE YOU? How long must this continue? Will I, too...Within my heart I can see happiness somewhere. All my dreams mustn't die. They can't. I can almost hear your prayers, Mom, they're calling for me but I can't come. I can't find the words to pray and to who or what? In the seminary it was easy. It was all laid out. My God was created for me, my prayers were created for me. Even my soul was created for me. Created for this? Where is my Sweet God?

Today we enter the lion's mouth and we carry with us the smell of death that I am sure will not leave us. Our mission, operation of death...sweep...a clean sweep...Ha! Like sweeping garbage!! I must stay at peace with myself or I'll go mad. I have friends; they are my companions and fellow spirits. I'm afraid to die alone, I can't! Ahead of us is but another omen.

Father, within my character is the candle of strength and I swear to you it will keep a man. I am a man, within the body of a man and that man will carry me through this. My fists are clinched and my jaw is hard, my feet are firm. Mother, I cannot pray if no one hears me and I cannot cry if no one cares and I cannot walk away or turn my cheek. I love you so...I guess it's all so simple now. It's all so clear. The whole theatrics of our parts, the dramatics, the stage setting. All the players are here. It means nothing and my soul torments me, but I cannot let it destroy me. It's the last great gamble. Just a roll of the dice, and my stakes are high.

—Franky

With the clearing of the smoke the whole valley settled like tranquility after the storm. All eyes stared intently towards the valley and not a word was spoken. Lt. Rich paced back and forth deep in thought with the strategy of our next move, of highest priority. We all wondered what awaited within the valley. The smell of blood lingered and echoed silent cries which grabbed at each man's conscience. The silence was condemning and we began moving about preparing for the next move into the thick brush ahead. Franky sat quietly by himself. He was scared and concerned like everyone, but somehow held a little more composure. Lt. Rich called in for air reconnaissance to study the valley and help us plot our best route of sweep. He wanted to make sure there weren't as many accidents as before. The valley was a perfect hideaway and vestibule for "Charlie" to plan his siege through our perimeters to battalions, air wings and even our hospitals.

It didn't take long for the Lieutenant to put movement back in our ass. He was anxious for air reports so we could move ahead. He had each man ready to move again and the next order.

"Davenport! Make sure you have all your gear

together and spread the word around we should be moving out soon. I just need confirmation from battalion and air people."

"They really did some job, didn't they, Lt.?" I asked with a smile.

"Yes, they move OK but so do these Gooks. You never know what they're up to or where they're at. They're like flies; we spray this whole damn area and they come out again. This whole valley is surrounded by hills, slopes, mountains and whatever. Somehow these Gooks keep filling in. We didn't have this much trouble before—it's getting worse. They're finally up to something. For a long time I wondered why they never made their move. Davenport, they go through this valley and through that corridor and they take a big chunk away from us. There's a billion dollars in equipment back there. There's medicine and God knows what else."

"But Lieutenant, don't you think headquarters knows it, and if they do, haven't they done anything? You know, to prevent..."

"Davenport, they haven't done shit. This war is fought like pussys with high hopes and political bullshit. Not like soldiers or fighters. That's why idiots like us get this detail. They're doing something alright. They're sending a group of hungry, stupid kids, like you, into this valley on a sweep which now they think had definite strategic merit, and if they die trying, well, it's what Marines are supposed to do. You know we're mini-supermen and if we get annihilated in this maneuver they'll move into more positive aggressive action calling it a *definite unwarranted, inhuman move* by the North Viet-Nam government. We, in the meantime, are victims of an obvious set of circumstances which could have been prevented!"

"What do you intend to do?" I was bewildered.

He glared at me with wonder deep in his eyes, questioning me without saying anything. Almost as if he didn't trust me. Somehow, he let me know it in his appearance.

"Davenport, I intend to do one thing and one thing only. STAY ALIVE! If you're smart you'll do the same thing. Now let's get everybody ready."

His conversation ended as quick as it began. He felt the hand was poorly dealt. Whether the deck was stacked against him or not, I couldn't say for sure, but I knew this much. If it was, he certainly wouldn't play a bad hand and if he had to he was coming out swinging. Still deep inside me I felt he had some master strategy which wasn't all his own, and that maybe we were in for something...something very unusual.

Looking over my shoulder I saw Frankly was by himself but ready to move out at first call. I thought for a moment of relaxing and keeping to myself, but the bug in me to talk to someone just wouldn't leave. Walking towards Franky I could see him squeeze out a grin. He looked like he was willing to talk.

"Hey, D'Amini! What are you doing?"

"What does it look like I'm doing?"

"You tell me. After all, I asked as a friend."

"Just thinking, Jay."

"Franky, you're always thinking, but what are

you thinking about?"

"Well, I guess I'm thinking typical GI, home, Mom, Sis, Dad, Friends, you know! Everything that's nice...It looks like we're almost ready to move, huh?"

"Yea, Lt. Rich looks like he's ready...What's your home like?"

"My home?"

"Yea, your home, or are you just being a wise guy today. How's your Mom doing?"

"Fine, as best as I can figure. Sis does all the writing. Mom's the silent type. She doesn't say much but when she does look out. She prays a lot. She prays enough for the whole family. When I was small we used to pray together, the rosary, stations of the cross. All that kind of stuff. Mom really got off on praying."

"And you?"

"Not anymore. I've had my fill. Practically had it stuffed down my throat. When I was small the nuns drilled the fear of God in me, not to mention the fear of them. I carried it right through school and eventually I believed in this monster so much that I figured not only was He all knowing, loving, and powerful but He was probably the best one to have on your team. So I joined it for life. I went to the seminary. Mom's dream came true. Her prayers were answered. Dad respected the decision, but deep down inside I could see he didn't think it was the manliest thing to do."

"You know, Franky, in some ways I could see you as a priest." I was smiling.

"Well I couldn't and it didn't take me long either. My friend Tom had a girlfriend and he was always making out with her and stuff like that and I really liked her. Her name was Gloria and, Jay, she had the nicest tits. Well, anyway, Tom was always telling me being a priest was faggy and how could I give up all the cool things in life, like broads, cars and booze. He was always pushing her on me saying, "Gloria, kiss Franky, come on, let him see what he's missing." Believe me, he didn't have to push her. Inside me I was dying to touch her and one day Tom was successful. After all, she was Tom's girl, but I could feel the chills as she turned to me and put her lips against mine. Then after a little while she stuck her tongue in my mouth...Jay, I knew then I could never be a priest."

"So that was the end of it, huh?"

"Yea, right there. The next morning I told Mom and Dad. Mom looked like her whole world fell from under her. Dad almost looked like he expected it, but I compromised. I promised to finish the last semester to give it more time, but I knew I wouldn't. When June finished, I was out for good. By that time the whole family knew I couldn't go through with it."

"How about your sister? How does she feel about you?" The more he spoke, the more I was interested.

"Oh, my sister is great. She always looked up to me. She's a little like me. She could never buy all that pious shit either, but she does a much better job of playing along with it than I did. She's very afraid of hurting Mom, but she's a great kid. She writes more than anybody and I can always expect her letters. She's going to make a fantastic wife for some guy. The perfect Italian wife. She's a little kooky, but level-headed deep inside."

"And your father? You never say much about him."

"I love the man with all my heart, but he's a silent man. A commanding kind of silence. I guess you could say he's a man's man. When I was young I could never do enough to please him, in school, sports, anything. When I looked to him for support or enthusiasm he grumbled acceptance and explained how it was part of growing up, being a man and not expecting banners or glory. I could never understand why he was so cold at times. It was impossible to get him to go to a ball-game I was in and there were many times when I could make a grandstand play and I had no one there to cheer, family-wise, but it was always expected anyway, and if I didn't do well, I was shirking my responsibility in growing up."

"Well maybe he wasn't into sports, Franky."

"Yea, he was when he was young. He was a good ball player and a good fighter. He was also in the war, WWII in the Pacific. He was wounded in the Navy as a Gunner's mate. I guess he's got his share of medals. He used to tell me about tough times during the depression. Boy, they had to hustle for a buck. I don't know, maybe that made him a little hard. He just seems unhappy at times. He's very realistic though, and that's one area where he helped me, especially now...hey man, you gotta tell me more about your family. You've been keeping yourself quiet and I've been rambling."

"Maybe some other time Franky. I'm just in the mood for listening and you're a pretty interesting guy." I wanted to keep the subject on him.

"Oh, yea! Real interesting. What are you—a comedian?"

"No, not in the least. You're OK. Guys like you don't belong here."

"Oh, and you do?" He came back.

"Hell no. Nice guys like me don't belong here either," I laughed.

"So why are we here?" He held up both hands.

"You tell me! You know why I'm here. I had nothing to do with it. But you, from the seminary to the Marines." I was looking for an answer.

"Hey now, I was only in the seminary for a year. After that I had a normal life like everybody else."

"Alright, but you still don't figure here."

"What's that supposed to mean?"

"Well, you just don't seem the type who gets off on war, killing, blood, you know the whole bag."

"Well, let's just say I'm a true American," he said smiling.

"Oh, come on, don't give me that shit. This isn't 1940. Now it's more American to peace march or picket or find a cause. At least that's the whole scene back home."

"You sound like you don't agree with it?"

"I don't know. Maybe I do and maybe I don't. Maybe I'm too much of an individual, and some of it seems hypocritical and just a wee bit phony.

70

Although I think some of it has good points. Just don't tell the rest of the guys, I'll be in the middle of a lynching. These guys would storm Iwo Jima again, but getting back to you. As you so cleverly led me away. Why you?"

"Jay, it's tough finding the answer. Maybe to prove something to myself. Maybe the challenge to stay alive, I don't know. I also wanted to get away from home. Mom and Dad didn't have enough to send me to college. At least not anything decent or full time, and I figured I'd use the GI Bill when I got out."

"Come on, Franky, that just doesn't sound like your best reason."

"No, seriously, I couldn't pin it down but it's a combination of those things. I just felt drawn to being a Marine. Maybe just taking the test of a man. You know..."

"Yes, I know. The kind of stupidity that gets decent men like yourself killed. You sound like you're trying to live up to some kind of image of a man. Either that or you're trying to destroy the image of a man you see."

"Maybe, maybe. It's getting so my mind doesn't know anything anymore. I do know this though, I sure as hell don't want to die here and I sure wish I was back home."

"My very feeling, Mr. D'Amini. My very feelings."

"You know, Jay, I look at a man like Rich and I wonder what he's really like. You know. The man inside the man."

"Yes. He's your prototype Marine, confident, strong, determined and most of all unfeeling."

"I don't know Jay. He seemed pretty concerned about Andretta and Budchinsky."

"Yes. He did seem a little concerned, but sometimes I wonder if he doesn't look at it militarily, a victory for the VC.

"Maybe he doesn't give a damn about Andretta or Budchinsky. Like a private war with him."

"Oh come on, Jay. He's everything a Marine officer should be. Hard, smart, gung ho. He's just doing what he's supposed to. I'm kind of secure knowing he's like he is. You know you can't be a pussy and bring these guys through, not to mention destroy Charlie."

"I know, Franky, but there's something else to him I can't figure and yet everything about the man is perfect for us and the Marine Corps. I guess we need more platoon officers like him. Have you ever watched his eyes, though, or the way he plans his strategy. It's deep and intense alright, which is fine, but it seems cold and vengeful. That man carries his own war, Franky, believe me. It's more than just staying alive or being a good Marine. He never talks much about anything to anyone...I don't know. Maybe I've been here so long I'm hallucinating. He's probably a prince."

"Well a prince he's not, but a good platoon CO he is. Jay, we gotta have guys like him. It's the only way we can fight this Goddamn war. You know it, I know it. I wouldn't want his job. I couldn't do his job."

"Franky, you're right. I guess a war can change any man. At times I fight my own self and feel the change. You know I don't want to become a shell before this is over. I want to live a normal life again and enjoy the same things, keep a lot of the same ideas. I still want to love and be loved. I want to cry and laugh...you know what I mean."

"Jay, you won't change. Maybe I'll change, but you won't change." He pointed at my shoulder.

"Franky, if you change, then I know we've got a problem. The world's got a problem. Just keep saying I'm *Francesco D'Amini,* Number One, Italian nice guy of First Platoon/Hotel Company. Okay Chief?"

"Yea. It looks like we're gonna move out any minute. Looks like the three minute hi-sign, into the valley charge the First Platoon. Thrills. You all ready?"

"Yea, but I left some of my shit over by Guliano. I'll catch you later, alright...and be cool." I walked away to grab my gear.

We were all packed and ready to go, everyone was alert and anxious. Lieutenant Rich set up platoon formation and briefed squad leaders. The valley was ahead of us. Our fears had to remain behind. Many of us knew that no matter what was done, the enemy awaited.

January 1.
Second Entry

I suddenly have the fondest memory of Barbara

Harrison. I remember how she was my first real infatuation. I loved her in those Mohair sweaters. All those nights I spent looking for the courage to ask her out. I was only 12 and so was she. But she was like a little woman. How I wanted to kiss her. She had a pretty smile. I even think she liked me.

I wonder what she's doing now. Probably married. She was so smart and had the cutest nose and chin. I wish I did ask her out. I wish I kissed her. It means so much now. As much as it did then.

—Franky

CHAPTER 7

"Souvenir Crocodile"

There were no more excuses and no further preparation needed. We were ready for our move into the valley. The air was dry and hot. The sky showed a soft blue and there were clouds in the sky, but the valley smelled of death. All the trees and brush were still. Our pace was slow as each man followed in order. We were well spaced and loaded down with gear. We had enough ammo and explosives to level the entire valley and I felt it this time. I tagged towards the end with Franky. He was slow to move but had strength in his face. A dozen thoughts bounced in my mind and all were frightful. The thoughts of home, Ginny and Jay, Jr., stayed with me. I had to cut them out of my mind. Thinking of home, instills even more fear of death. You act slower and think too much. Killing was fast thinking, and with little concern for extra caution. I, like everyone, had to shake the thoughts of home from my mind. My thoughts switched back to the valley. My feet in front of me watching each step, looking at each bush, keeping my distance and not losing the man in front of me. What if there's a mine with my name on it or a bullet? So what? You almost find you are thinking without thinking, asking without answering, because there are no answers.

As far as the eye could see the valley looked uninhabited, aside from a few small villages along the way and some small hamlets with no more than a dozen or so Viet-Namese. We followed an unrouted trail and were more or less digging our own highway. The entrance to the valley was behind us. It moved away faster and faster. Our pace picked up as we carried ourselves deeper and deeper. Some felt it was unnecessary to take the hard way in, that humping with all the gear would become even more unbearable. Some felt the fears we held were unnecessary. Maybe they were right, but we'd seen a lot more activity before than we had the past couple of days. Granted, we were getting hit soon, but it was still no indication that the valley was saturated with VC. The valley had been patrolled before. We had the same sweep before, there was always static, but never any major operation. Still the Lieutenant was worried and fearful and more calculating than usual. Even though he had been through the same sweeps we were, and with a hell of a lot more confrontations. So maybe he was punchy. Still the valley held major strategic importance, and up till now the enemy never really used it to their best advantage. The valley was a perfect mouth for spitting forces into the corridor which led to many of our most important supports. It also cornered one of our most strategic fighting points. If the Vietcong could secure Dakota and get deeper into I (EYE) Corps, their foothold of strength could stretch another 200 to 300 miles and serve as a strong headquarters for a greater assault on South Viet-Nam. Most of the men knew it, but no one was bothered by it. After all, they hadn't done anything before in all the years we were here. They made a few small efforts, but never a major operation. Rich felt we were due and maybe headquarters did too, and that's the reason for all the seriousness. The Cong feared our strength in and around the valley. We kept close tabs on any and all VC activity and if we felt it necessary, could declare the valley a free fire zone and kill everything in it. Our only problem was every time we leveled the valley, Charlie would spring up again out of nowhere as if sheltered from it all, and oblivious to anything we might do.

We knew there were sympathizers in the valley, amidst the villages and hamlets, but after every search and reconnaissance nothing could be found. No one ever knew anything. No one ever saw anything. It was the same story all the time. Maybe this time we could uproot something. If anyone was to find anything it would be Lt. Rich.

Cutting through the thick underbrush and trees made it difficult to get any perspective on what, if anything, was around us. We kept hoping that we'd find something that would give us a trace of a successful attack by our air support but everything was clean. Some of the brush burned with the aftermath of the rockets and strafing made by the jets. The ground and trees were black from all the rocketing but nowhere was a body or trace of Charlie's occupancy. Suddenly there was a stop in movement as Ferrara signaled for me to hold up. Some of the men left their positions and ran to the front where Rich and Johnson were.

"Hey Davenport, I think we got some dead dinks up ahead." Ferrara turned quick and motioned to me.

"You sure?"

"Yea. Come on, let's see what's up." He waved me up to him.

"Hey Franky, some dead enemy up ahead. Come on." I waved Franky up too.

We all moved fast to the front to see what was up. As I approached Sergeant Johnson I saw that there were some bodies clumped together, over in a small clearing leading towards a small hill. Lt. Rich was searching one of the dead bodies. He pulled out some papers, money and a small bag of rice. There were three of them but there were five AK-47's laying around them, along with extra ammo and other supplies.

"Johnson, looks like there were more than three of them."

"Yea, Lieutenant, that's for sure. They sure as hell didn't hump all this themselves, but I wonder where the rest went and why they left this behind?"

"There's a good chance they were just finding some of their dead and trying to move them when we came along. Hurry up! I want all these men broken into squads and dig up this whole area. We might have some Gooks breathing on us."   .

"Franky, come on with me and bring Davis. We'll head this way and keep your eyes open."

"Davis, come on, we're with Jay. Let's check it out." Franky called for Davis. A black Marine. A good soldier.

Everyone broke up into squads and began pushing aside branches, kicking aside bushes and digging into the brush in the hopes of finding something. Even though the area looked deserted we knew they could be breathing down our necks. I had Franky and Davis parallel to me covering everything five feet to the left and five feet to the right and keeping watchful eyes to anything else within reason.

Everything was quiet except for the moving about each squad made in searching to destroy our suspected enemy. All of a sudden we heard the most painful scream of agony. It wasn't far away, just a few feet, and it tore at our nerves. We ran to where the sounds came from and we saw the squealing body of one of our own men that fell in a punjipit. We all stood helpless watching what looked like Ray Guliano writhe in pain, like a helpless animal. The pit was no more than a few feet deep and sloped down, but the punjisticks were sharp and long and covered with animal or human waste and God knows what else. Two of the sticks stuck through his side and one through his thigh. His skin was torn and it ripped more as he fought to get free, but it was futile, as he lay helplessly caught within the web of the trap. No one moved. All were totally dumbfounded and struck with fear. The Lieutenant ran over with Reynolds and screamed for someone to help pull him out. He jumped into the pit and for a brief moment was confused as to how to move him. Then he pulled him loose with two other men and laid him on his back. Guliano kept screaming and moaning, and grabbing his stomach. The Lieutenant called for Doc and in a split second he was in the pit tearing away his clothes. Guliano was gasping for air and grabbing at his stomach as his whole body went into convulsions. It took all four men to hold him down. His eyes were wide and horrified and they stayed that way till he took his last breath. The Doc tried pushing air into his lungs with artificial respiration. He beat effortlessly on his chest trying to bring him back. But no results.

There was total quiet. Like frightened children we stood helpless. We watched a dead man who seconds ago fought desperately to live. Guliano lay there eyes wide and full of fear staring at us, like an omen of our own fate. An hour ago we traded C-rations and talked about the "world." Now Guliano was more than wasted; he was destroyed. For the first time I saw Rich look death eye to eye and death was now the master. He didn't move. He just turned slowly and asked for someone to pull him out. I was the closest, so was Franky. We looked at each other then slid into the pit. We each grabbed an arm. Franky let go and pushed his eyes closed. He had the same look in his eye that Andretta and Budchinsky had. A young, dying man unable to accept his death and completely overtaken by fear and pain.

We pulled him up to flat ground and covered him with a poncho. The Lieutenant ordered us to continue the search. Everyone moved slow, as if petrified of meeting the same fate as Guliano. We heard Smith screaming, "Over here, quick, over here!!" A few yards away the brush funneled into a constructed dome of leaves, branches, and brush. It covered a small opening. We scooted to the sides of the camouflage and Lt. Rich came running up with Reynolds and Johnson.

"Johnson, get a few grenades in there, quick! Then be ready to spray anything that moves." He stared at the opening.

"Ryan!!" yelled Sgt. Johnson. "You and Ferrara lay a couple in there. Martino, you and O'Herron spray everything in there, if it comes out."

In a second or two we had the three grenades popped into the tunnel. As the brush was kicked away, we heard them going off in muffled simultaneous explosions. Then we heard the screams. Two VC crawled and stumbled their way through the opening. The whole area became a blaze of gunfire as Martino, David, Ryan and Ferrara riddled their bodies. They bounced off each other and splattered blood. Then they fell in front of us, mangled in form like there were no bones in their bodies.

The noise settled down and the smoke of gunfire and explosion filled the air. Everything was still, except for the Lt. who immediately walked over to them and kicked them over. Two men walked over and asked for ear souvenirs as if they held some great collector's value. The Lt. just stared and shrugged his shoulders. Each man sliced an ear off with a bayonet like butchers, pulling off flesh of a dead animal. They carried their trophies and hung them up for all to see. The flesh hung loosely, dripping with blood. Franky stumbled behind me and choked to bring out what was inside him. Then I heard the Lieutenant.

"We're not done. Police this area and we're not leaving till I know we've secured it."

"Get a radio. I want a medivac in here and I want all this shit out of here. Smith, you and Ryan get Guliano wrapped up with his gear and get him ready, to put on board."

The Lieutenant went over the papers he had found and some of the men rummaged through the Gooks for souvenirs. He told us to recheck the tunnel for whatever else might be inside, then secure the opening. There were two more bodies within the tunnel and they were just as mangled as the two outside. The shrapnel from the grenades and whatever else might have hit them before tore deep into their bodies. We couldn't tell how long they were dead or if we had killed them. A lot of blood had crusted and a lot was mixed with dirt and mud and nobody cared anyway.

"Lieutenant, we got two more. You want 'em out?" Martino asked.

"No, take anything in there out and bury them with the tunnel. On second thought, drag them out there. We're sending them back as a little souvenir of this uninhabited valley!"

Martino yelled in his Brooklyn accent, "Crocodile, them mother fuckers!" (slang for kill). We certainly had a "souvenir crocodile," but so had *CHARLIE.*

CHAPTER 8

Keim-Lai, II

Within the hour another helicopter was seen in the air, reminding us of the visit paid just a few hours ago. There was a "Huey" gunship chopper behind her, giving support as she circled our position, acting as insurance for safe landing. All the bodies were neatly packed, with the gooks all together and Guliano separate. We all waited, expecting a barrage of anti-aircraft fire any minute, but the valley remained silent, undisturbed by their presence. The medivac put down and the "huey" hovered above, checking for activity around the medivac. We set up our position, marking the small perimeter with flares. A small squad hustled all the bodies to the medivac, and soon she was up and on her way. We picked ourselves up and headed back to our original position. The Lieutenant was ready to continue the sweep. He gathered us together again and rebriefed on the patrol into the valley.

"From now on, I want eyes and ears open. No slow downs and no slip ups. I want everybody to keep an eye on each other, but I want you spaced. NO TAILGATING! We never know what these gooks are up to. The whole valley could be smelling of mines. I can't afford any more losses. We still have this whole Goddamn operation ahead of us!" He was commanding and imploring.

Then he stood silent for a second and gazed at everyone, searching for a response. We were quiet so he continued to set down game plan.

"Let's face it. The Gooks are here and "Charlie's" looking for a piece of us. All the fucking rockets and shelling we throw at them isn't going to clean this valley. There's more to cracking this than shelling and reconnaissance—we have to dig them out. We'll have to breathe down their necks, like they're doing with us. Wherever we suspect Charlie we hawk him, whether in the villas, hamlets, or bush. They're starting to make a showing and if they pour into the valley like running water we've got to shut it off. It's a pain in the ass. We seal this valley off, blow it apart and they always come back. So the shit gets passed down to us, like always. This valley funnels into our own base support and if these kamakase specials filter in and breed an attack there's serious trouble. Battalion's oblivious. They feel stifled. They shell. They rocket. They blitz. They patrol and sweep. They shit all over this place and they still crawl out like bugs. We've got another platoon and an advisory post to make contact with. They're all a part of the same operation valley sweep and securing the valley, but I'd say we're the front runner. We're "Momma Bear" and we'll be spearheading most everything. We'll probably lead and call the shots as to patrolling strategy and reconnaissance and putting a lid on anything that's in the early stages. OK that's enough for now. Smoking lamp's lit. Take a little time."

We all stood around like orphans. The Lieutenant was a little more expressive than usual. He gave us some insight into where we were going and what was happening. It was clear we might be in for a nightmare and Rich was being straight with us. He was the type who wanted total dedication, so he spelled things out rather than leading us blindly. We had to muster all our strength and prepare mentally for what lay ahead. I felt a quiver and I probably wasn't alone in the feeling. Some of the older veterans had been through this type of thing before. They had an idea of what was coming and what to expect. They showed no emotion and seemed unaffected, but I still think we all felt the anxiety. We didn't know the exact details, but we knew more than before. Maybe the VC would fulfill a long planned dream, something that lingered in the air for years but never gained momentum.

I saw Franky's fear. His face was serious and hurt. He turned a glance toward me and stood motionless. I walked over to him and whispered, "You look like you have shit in your pants, D'Amini." He just smiled.

Everyone was smoking taking advantage of the smoke break. One always wondered whether it would be the last. I bummed a cigarette and brought it over to where Franky sat. I couldn't tell what was on his mind but I felt compelled to talk about it.

"Hey Spaghetti, I brought you a smoke." I handed him the cigarette.

"Oh, thanks Jay. I was just thinking." He took the cigarette and lit it.

"Yea. I could see that. So what's on your mind?" He took a few drags from the butt and passed it to me.

"I don't know Jay. I don't know anything anymore. What do you suppose Rich has in mind?"

"I don't know exactly. Looks like we're gonna make a clean sweep."

"Oh come on Jay! We're going to stop the whole North Vietnamese and VC movement. It looks pretty clear to me. They've got big plans."

I gave him back the cigarette. "We don't know that, Franky. I guess he's just assuming the worst to keep us on our toes."

"Maybe, but he looked concerned and he looked like he knew what he was talking about. What the hell is this spearheading shit?"

"I don't know. Maybe he's gungy, or glory seeking for first platoon. You know he's a jarhead's *jarhead*."

"Jay. You can keep kidding yourself but I'm not. We're not playing games. He's got something up his sleeve or headquarters has."

"So what. They've always had something confidential. What the hell do you think is going on? I suppose you believe Charlie's launching a major attack."

"I do! But not all at once. That wouldn't be smart.

They want to catch us with our pants down."

"So why the hell doesn't battalion reinforce, put on a full alert and support?"

"Maybe there's more to it than we can see. Maybe they want to get to the root of the problem. Could be they're avoiding panic which might cause major fighting and losses." He was feeling around for a reason.

"It doesn't make sense. If they're in jeopardy of taking a major assault on battalion, our air wings and all the support facilties, they'd initiate a major defensive.

"Jay you don't launch a major defensive against the VC. You play their game, as best you can. You try to out think them. You out sweat them and you out fight them, on their level. Then you have a shade of a chance."

"Franky, you sound like a military strategist! I'm proud of you." I patted him on the back and smiled.

He was still serious. "Jay, it's funny now, but you wait and see. There's worse days ahead, much worse and see if I'm not right. I hope I'm not."

"I hope so too." Nodding I turned and walked away.

I thought about what Franky said and whether he was right or not. If he was, what the hell could we do? What course of action could we take? If Charlie had any plans for something big, our efforts would be futile in slowing him down, no less stopping him. It was frightening. I hated to think about it, but Franky made sense. If he was right we had our hands full and I could see why a man like Rich would head the operation. For years Charlie controlled the jungle, fighting on his own turf with an unending drive to take more and more control. He was especially strong in the villages and hamlets in Dakota as well as in the thick of the jungle. He could very well be planning his biggest move but I made an effort to discount it again. Semper Fi was all I had to know right now.

Everyone was calm with the smoking lamp still lit. No one seemed on edge, with the exception of Franky and myself now. Most of the other men had conversations and discussions about subjects other than combat strategy, but it was obvious it was on their minds.

The time passed slowly and it was late in the afternoon when the Lieutenant decided to keep on moving. We were all briefed again, reminded to keep alert for mines, snipers and other threats. Our direction was due north about a mile or two for a hamlet called Kiem-Lai II. Kiem-Lai II was a small hamlet inhabited with 15 to 20 VC sympathizers, mostly old men and women and some children. Lately it was believed that the hamlet was an important stronghold for the VC in that many of their scattered forces were brought together from time to time in the hamlet. It provided an excellent access to the southern tip of the valley along with information from the villagers as to the latest enemy action and sweep activity through the valley. Judging from the distance, we would probably arrive prior to nightfall. The Lieutenant would most likely make camp outside the village hoping to discourage any more cong activity within that area, at least temporarily until we had restrengthened our main force. In a short while we would be meeting with third platoon and at that time we could coordinate our activity with theirs and layout grids and intelligence. This time I was more confident that we would probably interrogate and try to break the ville down into providing some vital information with the hopes that some of the villagers might have turned against the VC because of their treatment and some of the threats made by them, forcing their support.

"Let's move out!" was the call of the wild and my stomach instantly solidified, like cement. After a while we adjusted internally to the trials we met. We always hardened like a brick wall, so as not to be broken down or made soft. "Only strong will survive," rang through my mind. We all had to be strong if we were to survive.

O'Herron was put at "point" position. Mike was tall and wiry and had a talent for weird humor. The kind you couldn't understand at first but when you did you broke over into laughter. He could do impersonations of everyone in the platoon including Rich. He tried to be everyone's friend and never said a bad word about anyone.

Johnson followed Mike, with Martino behind him and Ferrara behind him. Then came Lieutenant Rich with the radio next to him and heavier weapons behind him, Franky was next, myself and everybody else. We also had four "ARVN's" with us. They helped in a number of ways with translations and unfamiliar Vietnamese customs. Two spoke fair English. We further utilized the ARVN's in the villes and hamlets for interrogation of prisoners as well as questioning important villagers. They were friendly enough and easy to get along with, but by in large they were poor soldiers, avoiding watches, playing sick at critical times. The South Vietnamese soldiers were not as dedicated to fighting the war as we were. There was one exception, KuChi. KuChi was a veteran, seasoned and decorated many times by his own generals. He was a sergeant in rate and could lead any South Vietnamese Regiment. He was tough and gave a strong appearance, although small in size like the rest of the ARVN's. He kept a close watch on his men and disciplined them when they showed weakness. He understood and realized their attitudes and short-comings. He would comment that it was common in many South Vietnamese soldiers. There was no middle ground with the ARVN's—they either showed oustanding valor and dedication or they weighed down a platoon. In almost all cases we kept the ARVN's grouped together, never tailing at the end for fear of losing them. KuChi played an important part in all our military strategy, in that he knew the people and the lay of the land, like the back of his hand. He even sensed moods among the Vietnamese people and knew when the VC were active in their ville. KuChi had two brothers who were killed while serving with the ARVN army north of Chu-Lai. So were both his parents who lived in a village about two miles east of

DaNang. The village hated the VC and was the victim of many of their vicious and unwarranted assaults. Many times the village chiefs would publicly display an execution of a suspected VC or its sympathizer. KuChi's father was a district chief and for years headed many movements against the VC. One night while sleeping, he and his wife were murdered with the roar of unending bullets. As if that wasn't enough, they anihilated their home with explosives and grenades making sure the job was completed. KuChi returned home that morning after being assigned close to home, only to find their bodies mangled and blown to bits. He was the last from his family except for a sister married and living in Long Binh. The pain within was so great from the shock of his parents that he immediately sought vengeance in an investigation of anyone who had possible links or knowledge of the murders. Inside of two days he had publicly executed half a dozen VC, sympathizers or suspects. He conducted the execution in the same manner his father had and he swore death to anyone who supported the Cong.

Our movement became slow and even more cautious than before. Rich and the point were stopping movement at every sound and clearing. There were no more bodies to be seen, but the thick of the jungle still lingered of the blood of probable VC kills. It was likely that their dead and wounded were already hidden or moved. For a brief time the jungle around us seemed safe and empty but the feeling of being watched remained.

Our patroling pace was more even and our stops

less frequent. Soon we were facing the small clearing that confronted Kiem—Lai II. Lieutenant Rich ordered half the platoon into the village along with Sergeant Johnson. The other half was to remain with him and make camp for the night. Johnson was to search the ville, hunt for tunnels and with KuChi's help break down information from the villagers. I left with Johnson for the ville. Franky stayed with Rich.

At first sight the village appeared harmless. Its only inhabitants were children, and old men and women. The entrance to the village was a dirt trail, rocky and sandy, with large holes and gullies. The huts were made of bamboo and clay. Some were made of coke cans from American supplies. The hamlet was poor and there was little rice production. The diets for the inhabitants was not demanding but it very seldom met with the yield the women and children could labor. The old men in the village sat around in idle conversation and were unproductive. Age among the men connoted respect or privilege. Their survival was their small harvest, together with the leftovers or supplies provided by either American or North Vietnamese forces, not to mention the VC themselves. Some of the women learned to barter their bodies for C-rations, medicine, candy, cigarettes or any item of value to the villagers. Horny GI's were always obliging. The VC compromised supplies for information and protection. They promised freedom from the miserable life the villagers eked out. They assured the women their husbands would return safely from some of the VC ranks once the struggle was over. The Americans were at a terrible disadvantage. The VC were more in control. No matter how friendly or kind the villagers appeared the Americans never trusted them. The thought of their deception always haunted us, that moment of betrayal or murder.

Looking at the village one would never suspect so much deception or enemy undercover activity. The facts remained though, that there were thousands of villages and hamlets in South Viet-Nam like Kiem-Lai II. These places gave the enemy the stronghold and support they needed to fight the static war it nursed for years. Here in the villes and hamlets the VC had their battle victories for it was here they made their grip on South Viet-Nam and squeezed till she choked. Here in the villes and hamlets our efforts faced doom.

As soon as we entered the ville a few of the children became active, running about, shouting and giggling. They approached us with surface smiles that implied friendship, begging souvenirs or candy and cigarettes. Some even propositioned for a lay saying, "My sister Number One Boom Boom, She do good. Souvenir, food, cigarettes. I fix. I fix!" Sergeant Johnson just pushed them off and KuChi would reprimand them loudly in Viet-Namese. The children would run off, some yelling profanities at KuChi, some laughing, some scared.

Sergeant Johnson was our Platoon Sgt. or Six. He was a tall, strong black man, a veteran from Korea. He was decorated and dedicated, a good career man, but a regular person. He had found a home for twenty years and it gave him a lot more than he had back in the lower sections of Chicago. He knew the Marine Corps but he also knew people and everybody liked him. He split our squad into smaller squads and left four men at the opening of the village. He ordered another squad with one of the ARVN's to run ahead and take position at the end of the village about twenty-five yards away. He walked with the rest of us through the center of the ville. KuChi called for the Head Popason and within minutes an ancient old man in pajamas limped his way to where we were standing. His left leg was shattered from incoming attacks of our own shelling, years ago when activity was heavier in the valley. This of course, added to his love of the American fighting and duty to the VC. KuChi began asking questions about the VC activity and yelled in a way that commanded response. Popason's answers were only weak mumblings of having little knowledge of anything. KuChi stared at him as if wanting to beat him right in the center of the street, but Sergeant Johnson held him back and ordered a search of all the hooches. He told KuChi to go with them.

We broke up and looked through the huts. Many were empty as some of the women and children had not returned from their chores. We knocked over rice containers, cases and some of the thatched furniture, but there were no weapons or documents to be found. Some of the villagers followed us in fright, anxious of what our actions might be. Some still followed trying to negotiate trades.

We realized nothing was to be found, there was no trace of the enemy. We examined their makeshift bunkers and found one small tunnel leading from a hootch that had been shelled and looked destroyed. The debris covered the entrance and if we had not been as ambitious as we were digging through the rubble, we never would have found it. Johnson ordered it destroyed. We dropped explosives and grenades in it and recovered it with the debris that was already there. There were no signs of life from the tunnel.

After the discovery of the tunnel KuChi began interrogating the old popason again. This time he was more emphatic and determined than before. Twice he knocked him to the ground and both times gave no further indication of a response. Popason kept pleading innocence and ignorance, claiming the VC had to have made the tunnel at night without the villagers' knowledge. Sergeant Johnson knew KuChi's presence was threatening to the villagers and warned him to surpress his actions. "We'll try to land more bees with honey," he said. KuChi grumbled and said he was foolish and that being soft would only allow them a better chance to take advantage of us. Nevertheless Johnson wanted respectable communication and he helped the popason to his feet. He told KuChi to make sure the old man knew once all the villagers had returned from their chores, he wanted no one to leave and that the village would be sealed off for the evening. He wanted full understanding. Anything short of full cooperation would result in taking prisoners or worse. Popason hastily agreed. He bowed and limped off, trying to avoid anymore attacks by KuChi.

Soon all the villagers were back. They all knew the Marines were staying for the night and that no one was to leave. It was made clear no activity was to occur. They all made haste to their huts and bottled up for night. Johnson radioed Rich, made report, secured our position and had us make camp. The other half of the platoon took position just across the way past the clearing leading to the ville. They too set up their perimeter with regular radio reports to us. I was placed at the front section of the ville along with Martino, Smith and Grayson. Grayson was with me and Smith was with Martino. We each had a corner of the ville. For a moment I thought of Franky, Rich and the rest of the platoon and hoped for a safe evening.

CHAPTER 9

Call To The
Night Brigade

As night came, we felt secure in our position. We all assumed the night would be free of any contact with the enemy. Even though the facts showed that Kiem-Lai II, like the other villes in the valley, was a VC stronghold, there were hardly ever any combat engagements in or around the close proximity of the ville. The Cong would never call attention to the ville, or threaten it, once they exercised influence there. It made for good relations between the VC and the villagers. We were hoping this would be the case and that no problems would arise during the night.

The hours passed and I could see the people in the hamlet shut their lanterns and make ready for bed. I heard some of the voices of the older men and women engaged in conversation, but soon, even their voices stilled as did the night. Everything was quiet and the darkness became more intense. It was a welcome pleasure escaping the jungle and the swamps for an evening. There, the mosquitoes hovered about you like low hanging clouds and made it impossible to sleep. The repellent we used sometimes helped, but gave an odor that got worse as you increased the applications.

Getting away from all that, not having to face the fears of the jungle in the night was deliverance. The jungle never communicated. It only stared and watched us. I never felt a part of the wild country, no matter how long I was part of it. I was relieved. My whole body relaxed.

Grayson looked steady on watch. He was a short, lean, good-looking Marine, with blondish hair. He always wore a smile, which is why he was given the nickname, "Smiles," by the platoon. He never said much and kept to himself. While looking at him, my last thoughts flashed to home and I was in sleepworld.

In the middle of my Shangri-La, I felt my shoulder jerking as Grayson wakened me for watch. I stared for a moment into nothing, slightly depressed for the sleep being interrupted. I still hadn't adjusted to the watches. I gathered together my senses and told Grayson to enjoy the sleep. We might not be as lucky, tomorrow.

Smith was about four or five yards away. He kept watch directly parallel to me on the other side of the ville. Smith was from a family of Marines, the youngest of four brothers. His parents named him Sam, after his grandfather, and I think he always hated it. Sam was dependable and honest. He was a good Marine and Rich liked him. He looked over and saw me relieving Grayson. He gestured an all-clear sign. I started to turn away from accepting his nod, and noticed his partner, Martino. He was out to the world, fast asleep. Martino was blocky, dark, wide-eyed and definitely I-talian. He was a big baby, always complaining, but never meaning any harm. The one thing he could perform professionally was sleeping. It was like rigor mortis. He would appear totally unconscious, with his mouth gaping open and his head back. At certain moments, his entire body would jerk, as if lifted off the ground, then return to its unconscious state. There was a time when we thought we could time his jumps perfectly.

The rest of the ville was quiet, with a squad situated at each corner, keeping an alert eye for VC activity. Every fifteen minutes, I made situation reports with the other squads and Rich's half of the platoon. No problems, my watch was to be a peaceful one. Then, with a chilling suddenness, I sensed something. My eyes travelled carefully across the clearing, towards Rich's camp. And saw nothing. To the sides of the ville, there were scattered trees and bushes. Some of the flatland in that vicinity appeared to drop off to the left about fifteen or twenty yards away. I directed every bit of my hearing to that spot. Nothing was seen or heard. Then I heard it again. This time it was clearer and louder, like the sound of a boot scraping on the ground, but still no movement or shadows. I reached over and touched Grayson's shoulder. With my other hand, I held up my finger against my mouth, signalling him of possible visitors. Smith saw me motion to Grayson and he knew immediately that something was up. I heard the sound again. This time more steady, like footsteps. There were no doubts. They were moving in on us. I couldn't risk radioing the rest of the platoon, so I kept quiet, pushing the safety off my M-16, pointing it in the direction of the bushes and trees to the left. Grayson did the same. I had my eyes fixed when I suddenly saw Smith turn to his right. They were probably moving in on his side, too. There was a strong chance they were all around, and if that was the case, it was better that we were split-up as much as we were. The sounds were closer and I could see a shadow. Then two. They moved inches as they slowly crawled toward us. Martino was awake with Smith's nudge and he fixed his weapon in the opposite direction I had mine. It was like ghosts in the night. Then it happened. I heard a voice, the sound of metal hitting the ground. We had incoming.

"GRENADE DOWN!" I yelled.

It fell just a few feet away, but the throw was bad and it blew in the opposite direction, with some small cuts whizzing around. We opened up and the tracers painted a stream of bullets into the bushes. They fired back and I saw the tracers coming from both sides. We yelled back for support from Johnson and the rest, but they were heavily engaged and needed support too. There had to be at least twenty of the enemy because they were attacking on all sides. The automatic weapons sprayed the entire ville. It looked like the Fourth of July. Soon, another grenade landed. This time it was more direct. I pulled Grayson and fell against the hut with him under me. It ripped past, cutting part of my calf, but not badly.

I grabbed the radio and screamed for some sort of illumination as their position was obvious, but not enough to make accurate strikes. We seemed to be firing into nothing. Rich responded and soon the sky was lit with dropping flares. At the same moment illumination exploded, the sappers made a dash for the ville. I twisted to let off a burst of fire. As I did, one came past me and we were face to face. It was only for a second, but we were eyes in the night, staring. I froze, but Grayson had a round through him before he had any more of a chance. Smith was pulling back and Martino had the M-79, putting it to good use and making hits, as the attacks from his side were slowing down. It wasn't for long. A grenade landed between him and the hooch. In scrambling to grab it or push it away, he ran out of time. The explosion threw him on his back and the whole front of his body was blown away. Smith was a few feet away with his face down. Their fire was nonexistent. I told Grayson to stay tight and I dashed across to help Smith. Some of the sappers were in the ville and I could hear the explosions behind me.

Cries of support behind me became screams of pain and death. All around was hysteria. It looked like we were to be leveled in no time. Smith was petrified at the sight of Martino and couldn't move. I butted him with my rifle hard enough across the shoulder to startle and move him. I screamed for him to return fire. Grayson was shouting into the radio for help. All I could see were tracers heading right for us. It looked hopeless until Rich's people finally made it across to us. Their fire support was hitting the enemy perfectly on both sides. For a moment their attacks stopped, as if they were totally puzzled and befuddled by the attack coming from the other side. Some of their fire redirected toward Rich. Some back to us. Some had stopped. Their strength was falling somewhat. I yelled for Grayson and Smith to pull back with me towards Johnson and for the rest to give support backing them up.

As we came upon the other three squads, they were still heavily engaged. KuChi was leading one side of the fight and Johnson the other. KuChi was directing the ARVN's and some of the young Marines as if he were a general directing his regiment. Johnson was screaming for illumination and heavier fire. They were lobbing in grenades and the explosions were cutting us down. Some of the fire from the VC was dropping off as they moved around to where Rich was pounding away. Their fire cut through and I could see one of the ARVN's bounce about as he became the target of a stream of bullets. They riddled his body and the tracers marked his place of death. O'Herron pulled away from him but he too became a target. He screamed at the top of his lungs as he still returned fire and fought back. He was on his knees and still holding when the fire formed a vertex on him, chopping him to pieces. He threw a grenade and had it in the air in time to do damage to the Cong where the fire was coming from. Then he bent forward with his head between his knees and stayed that way. He was dead.

Grayson still had the radio and was screaming for battalion, company, anybody.

"MY GOD THEY'RE KILLING US!" he screamed while crying, "THEY'RE ALL OVER US. PLEASE ARTILLERY, ANYBODY, ANYTHING!"

They were screaming back over the radio, asking for exact grids and location, but suddenly the fire stopped. There was no more fire or shots heard from outside the ville. We were still firing when Johnson ordered us to stop. Finally, everything was quiet. They were either holding or had pulled back. As we studied it, it appeared they had pulled back.

In the quiet, the moans of the wounded were heard and the smell of smoke from the gunfire and explosions made it difficult to breathe. Some of the villagers were coming out of their huts slowly. Their eyes were wide. The rest of the villagers still hid in their homemade bunkers.

After we were sure they had gone, we saw the Lieutenant with the rest of the platoon make their way through the other end of the ville. The battle was over, at least for the night.

CHAPTER 10

Fight On
And On

January 2.

Dear Diary,
The enemy has fallen upon us and like animals we fight to survive. The jungle has become a chamber of horrors and now the spirits of our dead walk with us. I was in total fear for my life but I fought on. I heard the prayers whisper within me but I refused to accept them. Now we must bury our dead and tend to our wounded. We must replan and regroup. We must forget and push on.

Our fate and destination is ambigious. I am becoming stronger but at times I find I am in awe of what is happening. My previous life becomes remote. If I die, I feel it will be unimportant. It will mean nothing. I don't want to die alone. If I do, not here!

The village is quiet. The air is still. Our dead and wounded lie all around us. Jay is alive as I had hoped he would be. So are some of my other friends.

Lieutenant Rich led us gallantly, dauntless of the enemy, blind to their attacks. For a few moments he was my strength. Looking at him I could see the total eradication of doubt or fear. He is a man like me, of blood and bone. We both think. We both feel. I try to be more like him, more like father.

Theresa has been with me each long mile. Her letters have given me hope. They have instilled humanity when it dwindles away. Maybe even Mom's prayers have sheltered me from harm. Who knows what the answers are? Who knows what the truth is? I have been spared another day. Maybe to fight again or kill again. I've yet to know or feel which is worse. To live for this or to die and escape. I push to be stronger. I analyze less. I am trying to ignore everything which I think is part of some absurd dream.

—F. D'Amini

That night we scattered around checking for dead and wounded. The count came, four dead and six wounded. Private Martino, Private O'Herron, Lance Corporal Robbins and Thuoc Pham (One of the ARVN's). Our six wounded ranged from demolished arms and legs to light scratches.

Rich was destroyed. For the first time he even appeared compassionate. He was at battle with his own feelings. He dragged about checking the wounded and talking to the Doc. He seemed to ignore the dead and ordered a few of us to gather the dead, covering them and keeping them some distance from the rest of the platoon. We lined the dead neatly and covered their bodies as ordered. No one said a word. Some of the dead were mangled. The others still looked young and alive but only sleeping.

One of our sister platoons was making her way to reinforce us. A "dust off" (medivac chopper) was on the way too for our casualties. Rich got together with Johnson and KuChi as the light of day came stronger.

"Johnson. This ville is the Devil's."

"Lieutenant, they knew we were here and had us by the balls," Johnson answered frightfully.

"You think I don't know it...KuChi I want the head popason right now. Get him out here?"

KuChi had two of the ARVN's get him. He was hidden deep within one of the bunkers. They dragged him out, his face written with guilt. KuChi screamed at him in Viet-Namese. He held him by the hair and struck him across the face. Finally Rich walked over.

"You little bastard. I want to cut you up for dog meat. YOU AND THIS WHOLE FUCKING VILLAGE! I WANT TO KNOW HOW AND WHEN AND WHERE AND ANYTHING!" Rich stared at him and pointed at him with a jabbing motion.

KuChi relayed the message so he could understand, but the old man stared. KuChi screamed again, but no response.

The Lieutenant was breathing heavy and his eyes were burning.

"YOU TELL HIM KUCHI. I'LL *KILL HIM*

AND EVERY ONE LIKE HIM IF I DON'T GET SOME ANSWERS FAST!"

Again KuChi tried to no avail. This time he tore off all the popason's clothes. The old man stood naked and scared. KuChi took his rifle and thrust it between his legs, jerking it up so the chamber and metal smashed against his testicles. He fell screaming and moaning while holding his organ and turning from side to side. KuChi was silent for a moment then pulled him by the hair. His rifle was still between his legs. The old man begged sympathy and rattled on about his ignorance of the VC and any other activity. KuChi didn't buy it. Again he jerked the rifle. This time harder and the old man fell again gasping for breath and pain. Rich ordered KuChi to put the popason with a guard, keeping him away from the rest of the villagers. He was going to send him back to battalion and interrogation, hoping their luck was better.

Sergeant Johnson looked worn and showed his age for the first time. He was tired like we all were and although he was stronger than the rest and more seasoned, he was fearful. He questioned the Lieutenant about the balance of our sweep and operation and whether we were to continue in the same manner. Rich answered holding steady as always.

"Johnson, we've got an operation ahead of us. This valley stinks with gooks but we're going to cut them off somehow. Battalion has to play ball with us. We'll reinforce and push a lot of these maggot stragglings out of here. We need more people with heavier support and better intelligence. We need hardened marines. We've got them here. We just need more of them and we need to know what's happening. Our battalion and headquarters can't or doesn't and neither do these cocksuckers in these villes. But I'll get something out of them. If I have to kick ass, I'll kick ass. I've had it. These goddamn little villes are a curse. They sabotage everything we do and come out clean. Battalion or Regiment picks up two or three of these bastards. Like that old popason. They push for intelligence and information and get some small bits of shit that doesn't amount to anything, but they're satisfied. Then they make them a "Chieu-Hoi" living easy and in the meanwhile we get all the blood sucked out of us here!" Rich looked at Johnson with apathy and Johnson sensing some of his depression answered back again.

"Lieutenant. We just can't keep taking these kind of casualties and we've got miles ahead of us."

"We'll hope they'll take casualties too, Johnson. From now on we'll keep one step ahead and we'll make sure we're ready for them. We'll try to cut off their communications if it's coming from these villes. We'll fuck their minds up somehow. No more short or casual watches and we'll double up on the patrols. I want killer teams rotating more and we'll sleep during the daytime if we have to. I want you to report to me on anything and everything. Same for KuChi and the rest of the men. I want to be told everything no matter how small or inconsequential. Understood?"

"GOT YOU! Loud and clear," Johnson replied.

"I hope so," Rich said firmly.

From the cut on my leg, blood was seeping through my pants, making it appear worse than it was. D'Amini noticed it and was playing Moma, insisting that Doc look at it right away. I tried to take care of it myself telling Franky not to make an issue.

"Franky, he's got his hands full. There's a lot worse than me."

"Yea, but you might get worse if you don't get that taken care of...HEY DOC OVER HERE! DAVENPORT'S LEG!" he yelled to Wesson.

"D'Amini, will you shut up. You big mouth. All I have to do is wrap this thing. It's no big deal."

It was too late—the Doc was over and before I could say two words he had my pants up and was cleaning my leg. The Doc was a fantastic individual. He was a Navy Corpsman but had become the marine's marine. He already had a purple heart and a bronze star, not to mention other meritorious commendations. His entire service was with the Marine Corps and he always could be depended on. The men knew Doc Wesson would die trying. Trying anything and saving anybody. There were many times when movement was impossible due to a surprise ambush or firefight and the Doc would still pull up and out at the call *"Corpsman!"*. He was good to talk to. He was a lot like Franky which is why they got along so well.

The cut on the leg didn't look too bad once he cleaned it and although it meant a purple, I couldn't see pulling sick to get out of the platoon. I could walk with no problem and the little piece that hit me passed right through, leaving no shrapnel in the leg. The Lieutenant was moving about, still checking everybody when he got to me.

"Looks like you've got a scrape there, Davenport." He was smiling.

"It's nothing, Lieutenant. I wouldn't bother the Doc but D'Amini's playing nursemaid." I tried motioning him away, so as not to worry.

"How is it, Doc? Any problems?" the Lieutenant asked.

"No. He's fine. Just looked a little bad at first, but it's OK now. He'll live." He was smiling too.

"Great—I need all the good men I have. See you later, Davenport." He waved as he walked away.

"Yea. Thanks, Lieutenant." I waved back.

The medivac chopper was circling overhead along with two gunships for insurance. They were scouting all around the area, waiting to hit anything in sight. As the dust off set down the sky was clearing and the sun appeared to be coming out more. We loaded our dead and wounded but no marines came from the chopper. There was no sight of new manpower. The Lieutenant was on the wire immediately to battalion. The dust off speeded away with the gunships. Our people were on board along with the old popason from the ville. They left so quick as if afraid of chancing our luck.

We wondered what was going to happen when the Lieutenant finished with the radio. He was talking to Johnson, KuChi and Ferrara. Then we were briefed on our maneuver. We had third platoon detouring to our position at Kiem-Lai II. Then together we were to join a convoy headed for Kiem-Lai. Third platoon had encountered much of the same activity we had in the past few days. Their casualties were great also, and their platoon size had dropped to near half. Apparently we were combining under Lieutenant Rich since their own CO, Lieutenant Conners was killed the previous day. Judging from their location they would join us within the hours. We looked forward to seeing new faces and the mention of the convoy was great news too. Taking the trip with the convoy made it somewhat easier at times. The trip was lighter humping since we stored a lot of our gear on the trucks or tanks. Sometimes we were allowed to ride. The only disadvantage was that it was a prime target for Charlie and now was no time to present big targets. Their hits so far had been more strategic with bigger numbers and if Rich's conclusions were right, they could be in waiting for something like a convoy with the platoons combined. It would be an important victory and allow them more control and access to the valley. In any event and no matter what the circumstances we still looked forward to the convoy and the uniting with third platoon. Now we would have a better opportunity of continuing the sweep. The only question that remained was how effective we would be against any major VC build up in the valley, and for how long?

CHAPTER 11

Alliance Of
Third Platoon

As KuChi continued effortlessly laboring for bits of information from the villagers, we packed our gear to make ready for our marriage with third platoon. Watching KuChi I could see his frustration. The villagers responded in the same manner the old man did. They played dumb or claimed the VC threatened them. Some insisted no VC visited them. Others just refused to answer. KuChi reacted with anger. He screamed and made threats. Sometimes he was overcome, like he was with the popason. He slapped them or knocked them down. Sergeant Johnson would intercede and warn him that he had to discontinue the violence. It was obvious we were getting nowhere with the villagers and that another night in the ville would guarantee even a stronger attack from Charlie.

Third platoon made her way into the ville slightly before noon. Her platoon number was about the same as ours, indicating she had met with about the same amount of casualties. She was as worn as we were. Many of the men collapsed as soon as they entered the ville. They were led by Sergeant Quirk. A big man from the South, who, like Rich, epitomized the Marine Corps image. He spoke with a slow southern drawl and looked straight through you as if questioning every word you said. He too was of the hero mold, being known to have charged several enemy bunkers during his tour. He hated the Viet-Namese people. All of them. As he put it, "You can't trust one of these slopeheaded dinks. If I had my way I'd kill all the little bastards!" In spite of his pleasant attitude he was worth his weight in combat. He was tough and shrewd and could outplay Charlie at some of his own games. He was the Corps' answer to "battle Sergeants." They were like old warships, being of value and strength for heavy fighting in certain types of battles, but they served little purpose and even became a burden in more streamlined, mechanized and modern military maneuvers.

The men in Quirk's platoon put up with his abuse but looked forward to teaming with us, especially since Lieutenant Conners was killed. Conners always managed to keep a tight rein on Quirk who resented it. Quirk was tough on the men and abusive. He demanded more than was expected and ridiculed those that were lucky enough to become his favorites. He did serve a purpose though, and for that express purpose Conners tolerated him. When Conners was stopped by sniper ambush all the men felt a serious loss, that is all except Sergeant Quirk.

Quirk immediately reported to Lieutenant Rich

and Sergeant Johnson, introducing himself as "Sergeant Quirk, U.S. Marine Corps, First Marine Division, Third Battalion, 7th Marines, Third platoon, Hotel Company and the meanest mother fucker in the valley!" Lieutenant Rich wasn't fazed and Johnson glared at him with the distrust a black man holds for big Southern patriots. His humor seemed to evaporate between Rich and Johnson, but Rich responded.

"I'm Lieutenant Rich. I'm CO for first platoon. This is my Six, Staff Sergeant Johnson. How are you men doing?" Rich extended him his hand greeting and Johnson followed.

"Ahhh, they're a little beat, Lieutenant, but nothin' earth shatterin'. They'll be OK. Seen a lot of shit out there. I imagine you've seen the same. You boys had a tough time last night, Huh?" Quirk asked curiously and in his slow Southern tone.

The lieutenant answered remorsefully. "They kicked the shit out of us. Took some of my best people. It was good we were split up. I had half the platoon across the way there." He pointed out of the village. "We helped close them off before they massacred the rest of my people."

"Get anything out of these gooks?" Quirk nodded towards the villagers.

"Nothing! They're VC dumb. They don't know anything and never see anything. It's the same bullshit! They're all VC. Their history is setting up our people." Rich was looking at the ground.

Quirk answered again. "Yea, we took a lot of shit just west of here and a little farther north. Over towards "Granitehead." Fucking gooks were like flies. Everywhere we turned, we were ambushed. In the day their snipers had a field day. We lost two men that way and Lieutenant Conners. At night they set up ambushes perfectly as if they had maps of our planned route of travel. There was no getting away from it and no breathing. They're out there and they know what's happening. The closer we get to these villes and hamlets the more concentrated they seem to be. They kicked the shit out of some "doggies" and "PF's" over by Kiem-Lai. Supposedly, they're crawling all around here, and those villagers are worse than these, Lieutenant..It's like old Ho's headquarters over here."

"I know. That's been a problem in this valley. We just have to play it smart and stay on our toes. We'll hang here for a couple more hours. Till your men rest up. Then we've got to catch up to that convoy on Mao's trail by 1700 (5 P.M.). Make sure your men stay clear of these women. I don't want any shit going on. They keep their cocks in their pants and no talking to these villagers. You got that Quirk?" Rich looked at Quirk for a second then turned to Johnson.

Quirk mumbled, "Yes sir, Lieutenant. You're the boss."

Then Rich spoke to Johnson. "You do the same thing. Spread the word. Villagers are off limits. *NO TALK! NO FUCK! NO NOTHING!* Tell KuChi too. Tell him I want those villagers confined to their hooches. They don't come out for any reason. You watch everything, Johnson. I'm getting some sleep for an hour or so. Get the men packed and ready to leave by 1500. Then wake me." Rich looked tired and sleepy—he turned to leave, and Johnson replied, "Yes Sir Lieutenant...Quirk, I'll see you later." Johnson turned with Rich and Quirk and flipped his hand from his head in a salutation of understanding. "Sure 'nough Sergeant...pleasant dreams, Lieutenant."

The Lieutenant finally bedded down for about an hour. With the pace we were keeping it seemed he would never sleep. Quirk broke up his people and examined the ville. He relayed the order for everybody to be ready at 1500. I sensed immediately that I didn't like him. So did Franky who rebelled at being called "wop" when Quirk gave him a detail. The Corps was made up of all kinds and we learned to live and let live. Quirk was no different than many of the D.I.'s in Paris Island. He had a personality only his mother could love.

Sergeant Johnson broke some of the men up into squads. He ordered them to check around the ville for wounded, or lame VC from the skirmish the night before. It was a useless patrol. The enemy seldom left behind her dead or wounded, but this time we were a little more fortunate. One of the squads returned with a seriously wounded Cong. He was shot in the arms and stomach. He was moaning and whining. Apparently he separated from the rest of his force and was too weak to move on his own. Two of the men carried him over their shoulders with his legs dangling between them. He was all but finished. His shoulders, arms and stomach were covered with blood. It was amazing he hadn't bled to death already. They brought him to Sergeant Johnson and KuChi for questioning, anything could help. All the prisoner could release were moans from pain. Soft moans made before the final hour. Johnson was searching for the Doc when Quirk walked over. He was curious and up to no good.

"Got yourself a sapper there, Johnson. Looks pretty messed up?" He had a devilish smile.

"Yea. He's not saying too much. He just about bled to death...I'd better get the Doc." Johnson turned again trying to locate Wesson.

"Hold on a minute. He might be dead before the Doc does anything. Let's see what the little fucker can tell us."

With his last words Quirk grabbed the VC by the shirt and lifted him off the ground, shaking him in a frenzy and yelling for him to talk. He threatened to blow his brains out. The prisoner never responded. He barely opened his eyes and made an effort to say something which sounded more like dry vomiting or coughing. Johnson jumped up, telling Quirk the prisoner was no good dead. Quirk darted back.

"Look, Johnson, he's no good alive either, if he don't talk, and the way he looks he ain't gonna be alive much longer. He knows somethin. It'll save us a lot of shit." Quirk wasn't budging. He pulled out his 45 pistol, put it against the prisoner's head and told KuChi to tell the cong he had five seconds or Quirk was going to put a bullet in it. KuChi did as told. The dying man just turned his head to Quirk, opened his mouth slightly trying to speak then dropped his head. He was dead.

"Sheet! This gook's dead already. Ain't no good t'all now and you was worried 'bout the Doc, Johnson." Quirk laughed and let him fall.

Johnson came back quick. He pushed Quirk aside and stared at the dead prisoner. "YOU'RE GODAMN RIGHT QUIRK! Maybe if we got the Doc we could've saved him, at least maybe a little longer."

"SAVE!...SAVE!...What the hell you trying to do? Save GOOKS OR KILL THEM? Maybe you're mixed up? The Corps tells me I got to kill them. Maybe you're fighting a different war?" Quirk answered sarcastically.

"No Quirk. We're fighting the same war, only different ways. You've got your ways. I've got mine."

"Are you a peacechild boy?...Why back home we think..." before Quirk could finish Johnson stormed back.

"I know what you think back home. Maybe that's your problem and from now on it's Sergeant Johnson, Staff Sergeant Johnson. Don't forget, Marine! And from now on you leave the prisoners to me!"

"Yes Sir, Staff Sergeant Johnson, Sir."

From Quirk's voice you knew he was being sarcastic and from that moment Johnson and Quirk had a relationship as good as any war we were fighting. Quirk always tried to outshine Johnson and Johnson was always controlling him.

January 2.
Second Entry

We prepare to leave. "Out of the frying pan...into the fire."

—D'Amini

CHAPTER 12

"Convoy!"

"C'mon let's get up! We're moving out. Let's get up! We're moving out. Let's get out of here!"

The Lieutenant was revived and anxious to move on to the convoy. The ville no longer was an escape or refuge from the jungle. On the contrary, it was a threat we were all eager to leave. We filed out in single formation with Country walking point again, followed by Holocheck, Lieutenant Rich, Sergeant Quirk and the rest. Sergeant Johnson led the tail end of the platoon with Franky and myself following behind him. Once we were out of the ville we started widening the space between each man. We kept a good enough distance from one another to prevent more casualties than necessary. In the event one of us triggered a mine or caught sniper fire, the distance helped strategically in a counter attack and also limited the losses in the catastrophe. Each man had to keep a watchful eye on the man in front of him so as not to lose place with the rest of the platoon. Occasionally in being over zealous about maintaining formation, the men got too close to each other making the man in front nervous. When that happened the man in front usually signalled for the one who was too close to push off or widen the gap.

We kept a steady quick pace. Franky turned to look over his shoulder from time to time to make sure I was following. He kept a good distance from Johnson and from where I could see, Johnson was almost out of sight. As we made our way through the thick underbrush and jungle, Franky continued to keep a strong distance from Johnson so as not to upset him with "tailgating." We headed northwest about twenty five yards from a small clearing which bordered us to our right side. Franky appeared puzzled and turned to look over his shoulder quizzically. Each time he darted glances to the left and the right, stretching his neck forward like a chicken. He quickened the pace while looking confused. Suddenly I realized....he was lost. He stopped short, swung around and held his arms up with a pathetic look that begged sympathy. He half smiled and frowned showing wrinkles of worry. In the clearing of paddies a few yards away there was a popason with a water buffalo, tending his crops. He wore dark pajamas. He was worn with age. Franky ran over to him as if asking directions. I walked up to investigate and see what had developed. As I approached them Franky stopped speaking and looked at me smiling weakly.

"Franky, what the hell are you doing?" I asked him in total wonderment.

"I lost Johnson about thirty or forty yards back and I was asking popason here, if he had seen a group of marines passing through...or ah...near...this...ah...clearing.". He replied slowing down while becoming softer.

"Oh Beautiful!...ARE YOU FUCKING NUTS?!?...Franky, what the hell do you think this is?...the information center at N.Y. Port Authority. For all you know this old man could be HO CHI MINH!! He'll send you into Hanoi FOR ALL you care. With a little luck you'll march us into the NVA High Command. No...we just stay put and hope Johnson sees you're missing and doubles back with the rest of the platoon or else we'll radio back to them."

I turned around and motioned to Valesquez to bring up the rest of the platoon. He in turn did the same and bounced his way up to where we were.

"What's de matter?" asked Valesquez.

"We're lost. Franky lost Johnson," I replied.

"You what?!...Oh mon! Chingao. How could ju lose him?..Eets not even night time."

Valesquez was funny when he talked. He was Cuban with the lingering Spanish accent. His round face and full smile made it easy for him to get along with anyone. He made the best of a circumstance or tough situation creating a joke out of what normally was a crucial moment. This time he wasn't jovial, but he did appear humorous while showing concern.

"Duvenport, do you have any idea where we are?" Manny asked.

"Not really...Why don't you ask popason...like

Franky. Then you and Frank follow the directions, come back and get us when you find the platoon." I stood there, quiet, with a smile from ear to ear.

"Right Davenport!..Dats a great idea!...unforjanately not for our side." Now Valesquez was finding humor and kidding back. I directed my comments to everyone watching to see their reaction.

"Look relax. We'll just hang on till they realize we're missing, then they'll double back."

"And if they dunt?" Manny was still concerned.

"Then we'll just radio them back," I answered.

"With what?" Valesquez was expressionless.

"The radio...don't...tell...me...we...don't have a radio...*VALESQUEZ* WE DO HAVE A RADIO...TELL ME WE HAVE A RADIO... *RIGHT?*" I asked hoping for the right answer. Valesquez stood silent for a moment with the dumbest look. Then he answered.

"Hey man! If you see one you're welcome to it."

I looked around. All that was left of the platoon were two ARVN's, Holocheck, Manny, Franky and myself...and no radio. I started to get nervous.

"YOU MEAN TO TELL ME THAT NOT ONE OF YOU SWINGING DICKS THOUGHT OF THE RADIO???" They all looked at each other not saying anything. Manny was beginning to smile, finding it funny. Finally they all spoke together.

"Well did you?"

"Well no...but uh...Manny you always followed...or...were ahead of the radio."

"Well not dis time. Looks like we just wait and

hope for the baste."

All I could do was look disgusted. Valesquez was blank and Franky looked down. Everyone else mumbled profanities or doubts in American and Viet-Namese. We had no choice but to relax and wait. If they backtracked, they'd run right into us. If we move they might lose the route we followed.

What seemed like hours were only minutes before Johnson returned to bring formation together. He looked angry and with good reason. He sternly told Franky not to lose pace or position. We couldn't risk losing any more time.

Country quickened the movement making way steadily to the convoy. Soon we could see the thick brush ahead taper off and lead to the open flatland just east of the Binh-Lai Creek. There was about half a kilometer between us and the convoy, assuming she made her way safely to the checkpoint. As it was in the past, many of the convoys faced harassment and sabotage by the VC throughout the valley.

It was not quite 1700 and we had made good time, even with the loss of time when our platoon separated. The convoy was in sight. She had not stopped but was moving slow. It wasn't a large convoy. All in all there were two tanks, three troop carrier trucks, half a dozen jeeps, and another half a dozen supply trucks ranging in all sizes. There were also about a dozen men on foot mostly carrying heavier weapons, M-60's, 79's, mortars, grenade launchers, LAWS. The troop carriers held Arvn's and PF's along with some of our own Marines.

At the head of the movement was Captain Reagan, a thin man with slight features and grayish hair but still youthful in appearance. He was a career man. Originally from Brooklyn, N.Y., he had moved around a lot, his whole family being career military. He had a slight slang of speech from N.Y. but he was a quiet man, short on words. His tour in Viet-Nam ranged from Commanding Officer of a Reconnaissance platoon to Executive Officer of a supply battalion. Reagan liked the field and the bush. He enjoyed the challenge and the danger. He volunteered to head the convoy, assuring battalion that problems would be minimum and that the supplies and equipment transported would arrive intact under his direction. Reagan enjoyed a good reputation, known to be a man of his word. He was cited for bravery on two occasions, both while on the same tour.

Lieutenant Rich reported to Reagan. He briefed him on the activity in the ville as well as the activity in the bush. They went over maps and papers, then broke off. Rich ordered most of third platoon's people to the rear of the convoy with Quirk. The rest were sent to the front to act as point and the rest of us followed along the sides towards the rear. We loaded most of our heavier equipment and supplies including our packs, on the tanks and troop carriers. We wasted no time and continued moving with the convoy. Unloading some of the gear and not having to untangle through the jungle, along with being surrounded by friendlies, made us feel secure and relieved.

January 2.
Third Entry

Not much time to write. Am happy to be with convoy. It's a welcome sight. For a few moments I thought I caused "Missing in Action" statistics. I have to be more careful—I can be more dangerous than Charlie.

C'AO—
—Franky

CHAPTER 13

"Mao's Trail"

The trail ahead of us was bumpy, dirty and long. Mao's trail stretched about five miles through the valley, then out again, heading north into North Viet-Nam. The trail was weathered from war. Over the years the mines, booby traps, artillery shelling and battles made the highway travelling unbearable. The holes and cavities in the road were snares for our vehicles. When approached at the right speed and angle the traps could easily overturn them. Our goal was to bring the convoy intact to Kiem-Lai to supply some of the small PF forces and the small outposts in the valley. It was from these small outposts that squads were dispatched for sweeps and patrols. Some acted as advisory units aiding our major forces and providing some security for some small villes and hamlets which had not become totally VC.

We reduced our speed as the road got worse, not chancing losses as Reagan had promised battalion. While walking one could observe some of the beauty of the surrounding valley with its graceful sloping hills and tall trees. The area immediately around us was not as beautiful. The small emaciated paddies, the rotted earth, around and beneath us. The total appearance of being worthless and war-ravaged. Every once in a while we passed a destroyed tank or truck, sometimes a jeep. They usually suffered their doom from hidden mines or sappers that carried explosives or anti-armor weapons. Once destroyed they were overturned and pushed aside, allowing the rest of the convoy access to the highway. They were like gravestones, warning you of the death that might lie ahead.

Of all the threats to a convoy, the biggest and most feared were the mines and sappers. Many of the mines were made from artillery rounds, 105, 106 or 155 millimeter. These were the most destructive, guaranteeing kills with any explosion. Many of the artillery rounds were neatly planted below the sand. In the jungle they could be anywhere, even hidden in the trees. Also feared were the "Bouncing Betties"— these jumped out when triggered and exploded somewhere between your hips and face. Once its prongs set off the small explosion which propelled its flight up, there was no avoiding it. The person at that point usually was in front of it and his or her back would be blown away.

Anything could set the mines off and usually it happened towards the point area. When this happened the convoy would stop dead. This was very dangerous because sometimes the attacks were planned, with the mines, not only stopping the movement, but disrupting it also. At that moment, sappers made their move. When attacking, they came from nowhere and moved swiftly, throwing satchel charges, grenades and automatic fire. They were quick, sly and their damage was great. Sometimes they would approach the convoy as friendlies, farmers, or villagers who needed help or showed curiosity, when in reality they were cong with satchel charges wrapped around their stomachs and under their pajamas. As soon as they were close enough, they would rip them off and hurl them. If they knew we were suspicious or cautious, they employed children, sending them over with orders to fling them when close enough. Sometimes they even arranged it that when the children approached begging for C-rations or candy, the explosive tied to the child would go off, killing the men surrounding it as well as the child. All these were common practices in the valley. The Viet-Namese within the valley were not to be trusted, for any reason. A fifty caliber machine gun was mounted on our tanks to prevent any such action. The men behind these weapons were given orders that no Viet-Namese was to approach the convoy. Man, woman or child, they were not to get within damaging distance. If they did and ignored orders to move away they were to be shot. Capt. Reagan was not taking any unnecessary chances.

Franky and I got into a conversation about sex while walking. This was one of the few times we talked about anything so frustrating. With the relaxed atmosphere and slower pace our thoughts drifted a little. Franky was getting cocky and spunky, making me wish I was anywhere but the Nam. He had a devilish look when he spoke.

"Jay, you know what I'd love right now?"

"No. Give me a hint," I replied.

"Two round, beautiful, soft...full...tits!"

"TWO WHAT?" I said.

"TITS! TITS! WHAT'S THE MATTER DON'T YOU KNOW WHAT TITS ARE?" He had a smile on his face that stretched from ear to ear.

"Yea. I know what tits are, but what a time to be thinking about them." He started again—this time his eyes were almost closed.

"JAY. I...can almost feel them." He had both his hands up and was squeezing as if he was really holding them, with his rifle under his arm.

"WILL YOU COOL IT!! YOU LOOK OBSCENE!" I said, looking all around me.

"What's the matter with you. You're human like me. Don't you like pussy?" Now he had his eyes open and looked at me curiously.

"OH!...I LOVE IT...BUT..." Before I could finish he started again.

"And pussy. There has never been a more beautiful thing created than a pussy. It's so captivating...sensual...and suckworth." His eyes were closed again.

"Franky, you're getting to sound like Valesquez. Now what would your mother or sister think?"

"WHO CARES! I'm so godamn horny my ears are growing." He slapped his ears.

"Yea, they look."

"JAY. Try and picture Joey Heatherton sitting right on my face. Those beautiful, beautiful thighs..." And again his eyes were closed.

"YOUR FACE? YOUR FACE? TRY MINE CHUMP...I MEAN...UH...WHILE SHE'S TRYING TO FIND A PLACE TO SIT. MINE'S JUST AS GOOD."

"Now Jay, you can't do that. What would Ginny think...I mean...you're a married man with children and all...you should feel ashamed..."

"D'Amini...shut up! Just shut up! I've got enough problems without being horny too. Try talking about something else." I was back to being serious, mostly out of frustration.

"I DON'T WANT TO! I LOVE PUSSY!" He just wasn't giving up.

"Well then go talk to Valesquez. You and him will get along fine. He'd love for the Corps to issue him a pussy for night watch."

"Oh you're getting to be like an old man. What's the matter...the little war getting baby sour?" His lips were puckered and his face chagrined. He was being the comedian again, so I decided to kid back.

"Now you know that's not true. I happen to love this war. It's the American way. It's exhilarating, challenging, exciting. It's..."

Just then there was a loud explosion. Up front. The convoy stopped completely. Reagan and Rich shouted back to stay down and watch the treeline. Quirk echoed the order. Everything was quiet and still. Nothing was seen. Then I heard shouts.

"LOOKS LIKE JOHNSON AND VALESQUEZ!!"

Franky and I ran to the front of the convoy. The smoke was starting to clear. They were screaming for Doc. When he got there, we could see it was too late. Both men were blown to bits. They were only a few feet apart. They had hit an artillery round. Looked like a 105 or 106. Valesquez was face down. His legs were stumps, with the parts that were missing some five or six feet away. His arms were mangled and contorted. His back was covered with metal and blood. Johnson was flat on his back. His legs also contorted behind his back. His face was indistinguishable. His right arm was gone. Country stood over them crying. He liked Johnson...and Valesquez was his good friend.

Our original platoon was now down to a handful of Americans and three ARVN's. In the past few days we had taken more casualties than the entire company. Our dead numbered ten, our wounded seven. Captain Reagan radioed for a "dust off" to pick up Johnson and Valesquez. Everyone felt the loss of Staff Sergeant Johnson and Private Manuel Valesquez. Both had become an important part of the platoon and our way of life. All spirits were low and tension within the platoon was rising. The enemy was breaking us down piece by piece, day by day, man by man. Everyone wanted confirms. We needed to confront the enemy and drive them down. We wanted our tormentor face to face.

Our medivac chopper was in and out fast. News had made its way back to battalion, that the valley was becoming a cemetery and that our normal patrolling maneuvers were taking heavy casualties.

They suspected there was a build up of VC within the valley and that more forces and support was needed to do the proper job but they still dragged their heels. They claimed there was no substantial proof yet, to warrant reemploying troops already tied up and concentrated in other areas. They only committed to promising more support than usual if the attacks continued along with the data they were accumulating about the valley.

Captain Reagan knew the men were on edge. He decided to continue the convoy for another three/quarter of a kilometer, where the area would be more secure. The trail ahead of us turned west a little, just past some clumps of dirt and brush. There the road offered more security. There was no access to it without being detected. Once past the small hills, everything was clear.

Everyone was quiet. Hurt was written all across first platoon's faces. As we turned the corner we spotted farmers tending their fields. They were only a few yards from the highway. There were about a dozen, men, women and children. Captain Reagan ordered KuChi to get them away from the convoy.

"DI OI! DI OI! DUNG NOI! DUNG NOI!" KuChi screamed. Quirk echoed the same command in his Southern drawl.

"DI DI MAU YOU FUCKIN GOOKS OR WE'LL FLUG YOUR ASS?"

No sooner had the command been given then two of the children dropped everything they were doing and started making their way towards the convoy. Then one of the farmers and an old woman followed. Reagan yelled.

"KUCHI *GET THOSE PEOPLE TO STOP OR WE'LL OPEN FIRE!!*"

Again KuChi yelled. "*DI OI! DI OI! DUNG NOI!*"

The children looked innocent. They were mumbling something in Viet-Namese. Some of the women were starting to edge closer also. They were only a few yards away when the order to open fire came.

The tank men bore down with their fifty calibers and let go. One bullet hit the first child then the popason. The child fell to his one knee as the bullet hit his leg. While falling he unwrapped a satchel, hidden on his waist, and hurled it towards the tank. It failed to explode. The second child got within feet of the Command jeep and threw a grenade which landed directly in the jeep, throwing Reagan and his men clear of it. The tankmen couldn't hold back as they sensed the danger. They opened up on the rest of the farmers. This time they were more accurate. They killed two women and another old popason. The rest fled for their lives.

We all watched as if spectators for the first time, not having to fire a single shot. Our Corpsman ran to Reagan to see how bad he was hurt. He was lucky. He bought a ticket home. He had shrapnel in the leg, arm and back but nothing that would kill him. The rest of his men were not as lucky. The two men in the jeep were finished.

Lieutenant Rich ordered a halt to the convoy movement. He took over command since Reagan was bleeding heavily and appeared semi-conscious. He grabbed the radio and called for another medivac.

"Hotel Head. This is Hotel One. Request urgent dust-off. Sappers! Sappers! Have Moma Bear winged with two DOA's. Grid 416182SL. GET IT MOVING! I repeat MOMA *BEAR WINGED WITH TWO DOA's GRID 416182SL. NEED FAST!!*"

Rich then ordered a squad of four to check the dead Viet-Namese. The first child was only wounded. He spoke nothing and carried nothing but the satbchel charges he tried to land on our tanks. The old popason was dead. Strapped to his stomach were grenades, pistol and a knife. There were no maps or papers on both bodies, just the weapons.

The two women and the old popason were not as heavily armed as some of the others but the old popason had a carbine rifle strapped to his side and covered by his pajamas. The barrel of the gun ran through his pants, pointing at the ground. Each of the women had a grenade. All three were dead. We piled all the bodies and wrapped our dead. The medivac was quick again. It was as if they ran a shuttle for us. We loaded all the dead and placed Captain Reagan and the wounded child on board. In moments it was on its way.

With the Captain medivaced and gone, the Lieutenant had his hands full. He decided to secure, have us rest and plan for the next day...night was approaching.

CHAPTER 14

Remonstrance Of Character

Our night was peaceful and still, unlike each day before. There was no movement or even a trace of the VC. The men slept soundly, although anxious and nervous at first. The marching and fighting had worn them thin. The morning was a pleasant relief. The sky was hazy and slightly overcast but there was a light current of air passing through the clearing that was refreshing. The Lieutenant was awake but in no hurry. He looked at maps, paced and occasionally talked to Quirk. Rich didn't appreciate Quirk, but in the past few days losing Johnson, Reagan, and two squad leaders, Quirk was all that was left. According to battalion third and first platoon had merged temporarily with Quirk as platoon Sgt. and Rich CO. Third platoon was being replaced in entirety and was to make its way into the valley to aid in operations and future sweeps. Battalion hadn't promised when. Rich was hoping soon, particularly with continued action in the valley.

With all the excitement in the preceeding days we were holding our position calmly and with no rush to faciliate our movement to Kiem-Lai. The morning was spent in relaxation, writing letters, having coffee and conversation, some catching extra shut eye. Rich was making rounds, boosting morale, checking supplies and familiarizing himself with some of the new platoon members. Franky was writing as usual. He was by himself, away from the rest of the platoon and avoiding conversation. Whenever Franky wrote, whether letters or diary, he made sure he had the solitude that allowed him to enjoy the thoughts he so dearly treasured.

January 3.

Dear Diary,

This morning I wrote Theresa and Mom. I wrote a few lines to Dad. I can never say much to Mom or Dad except to send my love. I do love them. No matter how hard I try I never really know what to say to them. Everything here is so unbelievable. Most of it I can't tell anyway. If I wasn't here I wouldn't believe it myself. At times I feel compelled to tell someone, other than the people here. There's some sanity out there that needs to be told. I don't want sympathy or affection. I seem to want answers as if someone were to blame for never telling me about this. I wonder if they knew and if they don't, should I be the precursor of this circus. Can humanity allow what is happening? Can it change? Where do our values lie? What does the future hold?

Are some more innocent than others? Or are we all guilty of the same crime?

Today will pass like the pages of this diary and tomorrow holds the same story if no one cares. We preach love and manufacture hate. We tell our children nursery rhymes with happy endings, with heroes and heroines but we still don't tell the whole story. We leave out the part that is the most unpleasant, but the most realistic.

"Everyone's gone to the Moon." I seem to hear those words from a song I use to sing. Now they no longer are pretty words. They no longer ring like beautiful music. "Everyone's gone to the Moon," except the children of damnation who sweat and die here. It is said the greatest fear is that of the unknown. That could not have been said, save only in the absence of war. I hope I continue to live and write, for my writing is that of my sisters and brothers who cannot. I face my doubts each day and my shame each night when I close my eyes to rest my body and meet my spirit.

My words have become useless, like the poetry within me.

Echoes of those fallen, have touched deaf ears.

Thoughts of those thinking, have rendered no tears.

Images of doom are confronted with sighs.

Posterity's no gain, as each of us dies.

—D'Amini

After evaluating the convoy's losses, Rich felt

confident we would make good time and be at Kiem-Lai within a day's travelling. His only problem was the temperament of the men within the platoon. Many had gone sour. The atmosphere was calm but the men felt anxious and uncontrolled. Rich needed to maintain strong control. He needed to unite the men under a common desire to stay alive and still perform as Marines. The bulk of work still lay ahead. First platoon needed to gather intelligence at Kiem-Lai, strengthen the Popular Forces, unite with any additional troops sent to continue sweeps and patrols around the village. The VC were gaining, not only control of Kiem-Lai, but all the villes and hamlets in the valley and now the valley itself. Kiem-Lai offered the biggest challenge. The village was considered a near impossibility in reversing the VC action. As in the past, it acted as the VC refuge and intelligence machine. The South Viet-Namese Popular Forces and propaganda had lost a long struggle to gain support. Much of their forces had deserted or been killed by the enemy. Those that were left, acted and united with American forces that served in an advisory capacity.

The danger within the village was so great they eked an existence in small outposts hidden within the valley and near the villages. Some of the small American squads and platoons had been spared only because they were considered no threat and at times even aided in the intelligence gathered by the VC within the ville from the inhabitants. Sometimes they even broke down feartorn and defected PF's.

To the VC the village was impregnable and now they were more active than ever, moving at accelerated speeds to capture the valley and push further on. The South Viet-Namese and American Propaganda machine had failed. Hope rested in the operations and aggressive actions of the U.S. Marines. Rich saw these as the facts. He only hoped First platoon could be effective and not totally destroyed at the same time.

Rich and Quirk met with some squad leaders. They prepared strategy and platoon unification for the move to Kiem-Lai. While the platoon leaders were engaged in conversation so were the men in the platoon. The conversation headed around where we were going, what we were doing and what chances there were of any of us making it alive. Country and Holocheck were the most expressive with Ferrara and Davis giving fuel. Franky and I were spectators more than anything, weighing what was said. We hoped most of it was just frustrations and tensions. Poor attitudes were always the enemy's best weapon. Country, who normally limited his vivacity to smoking a joint or doing personality impersonations, showed a different side. It seemed to attribute from the loss of Sergeant Johnson and Valesquez, his two friends.

"This maneuver is suicide. Before you know it, we'll all be wasted!!" he said.

"Yea. Johnson's gone now! He never knew what hit him. He was no kid either. Gave a lot of years to the "Crock" and in a few seconds all it got him was a body bag!" Holocheck answered.

Both men batted it back and forth, mostly repeating the same things. Then Pete Ferrara the well built Italian, otherwise nicknamed "Bruno" chimed in with Davis, a slender black man from Kentucky.

"Well...What the fuck are we gonna do? Things aren't cool at all. You know Rich, he's gung ho Marine Corps."

"No shit, Ferrara. He's gonna make sure he gets a Silver Star this time. That is whether we're around or not," answered Davis.

Franky couldn't hold back. He spoke up before things went any farther.

"Listen, Rich is just doing his job. It's not easy right now!"

"The best thing he could do is to get our ass out of here and have them blow this valley away!"

"Right Davis, and how to you propose he do that?" asked Franky.

"Get some chopper to get us out of here. The fucking valley ain't worth all our lives."

"Yea and how many lives will be lost if we just give up?" Franky was firm.

"Hey man. We're shit next to these gooks. They know our every move. They're all over the place like flies. They're in the paddies, the jungles, the villes, they're all over."

"Well, we'll be getting more people soon," said Franky.

Davis was aggressive now and unbending. He made a point and intended to drive it home.

"What People? WHEN?"

"Soon Man. Soon."

"Soon shit D'Amini. I want to know when?"

"I don't know but...he'll get support."

"Hey man. Get wise. He don't know either and if we got to fight this war single handed he'll try and do it and do you think we CAN?"

"WELL what do you suggest, Davis? He's the best thing we've got right now." Davis looked at Franky not giving an answer.

"Franky's right, Davis. Rich knows his shit and if anybody can pull us through, Rich can." I couldn't resist coming to Franky's defense. He was right. Country was quiet but Ferrara still agreed with Davis.

"Listen D'Amini. All the guys agree. It looks pretty sad and if something good don't start happening, we got problems, serious problems."

"Well look, it's not too much farther to Kiem-Lai. We hold out for a while, relax, reinforce, then move back on our sweep and get relieved. Then it's back to battalion for some hot chow and new scenery." Franky made it sound simple, but "Bruno" came back again.

"Oh Yea! That's pretty if that's the way it is but that's not the way it is. That fucking ville is getting worse than this bush. They're all Cong. They've been giving shit to our people in and out of that place. What the fuck are we gonna do there? PLAY WITH OURSELVES? And if we don't get more manpower and firepower fast, how long do we hold out? What about the stinkin valley when we sweep back, if it's filled with Charlie, HUH?"

"Ferrara, this goddamn war was never meant to be simple. We've got a lot of shit to smell for a while but we'll pull through. Rich knows what he's doing. The man's confident. He's not stupid."

"Maybe he's confident but he sure don't look healthy lately. Did you check him out?" he asked.

"So? He's beat. We all are."

"Franky, I hope you're right. These gooks are getting to me. I want blood like anybody else but not mine. It's anybody's guess who and where they are. Like those farmers and women and the kids. Shit man, they might as well wear NVA uniforms. The people in this valley are the enemy. We got no more control over them. They want it all now."

Country was quiet for a while then he came back into the conversation only to express his initial feelings.

"Valesquez, Johnson, Guliano, Martino and all the rest. I just can't see it. What an awful way to go. I don't want that action. I'm not afraid to say it. Ever since Valesquez and Johnson I get these chills down my back. It's spooky and like...I've been here for a while so I'm no newbee (new man). If we fight it out that's different—I can get a piece of that. I can taste that but this action is frustrating to say the least."

"Listen Country. If you guys feel that strong about his, why don't you talk to Rich." Franky was trying to find a solution. Davis jumped in.

"Are you nuts? He's all Marine Corps. He'd start wondering where your head's at. Then you'd be on his shit list. NO way man! We got enough problems without having Rich pissed."

"Well then, drop it. There's nothing major to do. Just keep your eyes open and listen to the guy. Believe me. He's on to what's happening. He's the best I've seen. We're just getting more shit than usual. Look, maybe I sound gungy but we're "grunts"—we're supposed to be made for this shit. We gotta get tougher and less petty. Sure it's bad but talking about it isn't going to make it better. Jay feels like I do, we'll pull through. Somehow..." Country came back and cut Franky off.

"D'Amini you sound good. Let's see what happens and how far we get. But for Johnson and the rest I do hope we take a shitload of these gooks...the little bastards!"

Country was firm and so were the rest. The situation was bad. Our casualties were high and things didn't look like they were going to improve. Country, Ferrara, David and Holocheck were expressing what many of the men were feeling and arguing did little to settle their nerves. They wanted escape or blood. It was starting to look more like blood. Inside I hoped Franky was right.

January 3.
Second Entry

The men are tired and hurt. They're all strong men—especially Ferrara and Country. Ferrara has conviction and feeling. He fights hard and he's a lot like Rich, in appearance and actions. I hope he understands. I grow to love them all.

We need Rich now. Nothing is easy. We struggle

everyday. We can't give up hope.

Jay becomes a better friend everyday. He has the curious eyes of my sister, the sandy hair of my mother and the quiet strength of my father.

—Franky

CHAPTER 15

"Fort Number One"

Soon we were back on our way, making greater speed than before, trying to avoid the constant exposure on Mao's trail. Rich was determined to make Fort "Number One" before nightfall. Fort Number One was a small fortress occupied by a dozen PF's and less than half a dozen American advisors. The advisors were mostly Green Berets or Rangers acting in a support advisory capacity. Their team was headed by Sergeant O'Donnell, a tall stocky young man with little actual combat time. He had an excellent record and was chosen as replacement for Sergeant Thomas—another New Yorker who was killed on Night patrol with three of his own men and two PF's.

The fortress was well situated, just north of Kiem-Lai about half a kilometer. The fortress was well camouflaged within the bush. She sat on a small hill overlooking the paddies which led to Kiem-Lai about half a kilometer away. The fort was almost inaccessible except in a full scale attack. It was well surrounded and protected with concertina wire and their own booby traps which on more than one occasion proved successful in discouraging the enemy from minor attacks. The Popular Forces within the fort were not all from Kiem-Lai. Many had come or were ordered from other surrounding villages. At one time Kiem-Lai supported a large PF force but over the last several months in becoming almost entirely VC, their PF's either switched sides, fled, suffered torture or death. Things were so bad the existing PF force remained entirely within the fortress, seldom chancing their existence in Kiem-Lai.

Those that had family within the PF ranks were scarce for many had been killed along with the militia. Those that remained were harmless and caused little aggravation for the Cong representation.

The PF's had named the Fort from the common slang used in Viet-Nam in referring to *quality*. On a scale of "One" to "Ten," *"one"* was the greatest, *best, tops!* *"Ten"* was the *worst, bottom, end.* Many times they referred to American troops as "Number *One*" and VC, "Number *Ten!*"

With the friction in the village and the build-up around the valley, the PF's and Americans there made minimum visits to Kiem-Lai and only during the day. They suffered heavy casualties like we had in the proceeding days and were frightened as to their outcome also. They had also radioed for support and reinforcements or an immediate pullout. Things seemed fairly hopeless. The men there were anxious to meet our platoon and they were in nervous anticipation for supplies. They had limited their patrols in fear of the VC concentration but still continued to send out some night teams in surveillance of the enemy. They didn't need to search far. In each instance, they either met with the enemy, or pulled back to avoid conflict with their much larger numbers. Their job had become too large and their effect on the village or enemy activity was almost meaningless even though at one time their killer teams were a threat to any Cong night patrols.

We came upon the fortress late in the afternoon, near evening. It looked haunted and old, made of clay and cement, covered with brush and wooden planks. The roof hung over the sides and held sand bags which absorbed some of the blasts and shrapnel from incoming. The concertina wire was old and worn from the monsoons and previous battles. There were small bunkers on each side of the fortress and another lookout bunker near the front, a few yards from the entrance on the gate. Behind the fort was brush and a drop off that was heavily mined to prevent rear attacks.

We stood ground from the fort, about twenty yards away, waiting to be escorted formally so as not to set off any welcoming traps. The convoy laid in waiting and eventually Sergeant O'Donnell made his way down to Lieutenant Rich and welcomed him. O'Donnell gave a salute and Rich returned. Then O'Donnell eyed the tanks and trucks gleefully as if we had brought him half the whores in China.

They exchanged a few words before turning to the fort.

"Lieutenant, those tanks and goodies for us?" O'Donnell still carried the grin.

"I'm afraid not, O'Donnell. We got some PF's for you, some ammo, frags, maps and rations. The rest of these people and vehicles were acting as support for us, then they're heading south to give some localized shelling for the other PF camps, resupply them, then back to battalion."

"You mean all we're getting are some PF's?!??" Disappointment was written all over his face.

"Looks like that's it, O'Donnell, till something else comes up."

"Lieutenant, you don't know what it's been like out here. They're coming in like open house and kicking our ass. There's no telling what they're doing. We could be gone tomorrow. Our Division and your Battalion thinks we're "short time sick" (Phrase for short time left in duty) and just making our usual normal amount of contacts. That there's no big deal. Same as always and I'm the new guy who's making all the problems, raising all the eyes. Well, let me clue you in..." Rich cut him off.

"*Listen O'Donnell,* I know what it's like. I've got more casualties than men. It's taken two strong platoons to make one weak one and that's what I've got now. Don't you think I'm giving them the same shit. They can't be oblivious forever. They're going to start sending reconnaissance and troops. We've just got to contain and hold. You people are a big help. You know the land, the people, even the enemy. That's important. We should pick up forces soon, secure this village, and sweep back through the valley."

"That's fine Lieutenant. Depending on what they have in mind. We estimate at least a regiment filtering in already."

"THAT MANY?" Rich had a surprised look.

"At least. The only reason they haven't taken our fortress yet is because they don't want to draw attention and they don't consider us a threat...AND WE'RE NOT!"

"Look we'll go over this more. Let me secure my men and get some of this stuff unloaded...QUIRK!" He turned, looking for him.

Quirk was slow in responding and dragged feet up to the Lieutenant.

"Yea, Lieutenant."

"Quirk, get the men to unload the trucks and secure. Who's your best man?"

"Why...uh...Corporal Tucker. He's been in country the longest and he's about the toughest. He's a good Marine knows his shit, in fact he was a Sergeant few months ago, 'cept he got busted for drinking...nothin dramatic just a stripe..."

"Quirk, never mind all that. Is he good? I'm gonna put him in charge of the rest of these trucks and things till they get back to Kiem-Lai II. Lieutenant Williams will probably pick it up from there and I don't want any problems."

"Oh, no problems, Sir. He's the best under fire and commands respect. He's the oldest next to me. He knows his grids, the land and he's good."

"OK. Get those trucks unloaded, and send the rest back. Tell him I want hourly reports and no trouble...He should be alright—he's got enough fire power."

"Yes, Sir, Lieutenant. Take care of it right away." Quirk walked back down.

Tucker was good and he took control right away under Quirk. We unloaded rations, explosives, ammunition and weapons along with the PF's assigned to Number One. O'Donnell and Rich went inside. The PF's stationed at Number One helped out. Some knew the PF's we had with us and immediately started to rattle off Viet-Namese about what's what who's who. Quirk was annoyed with the heavy jabber and ordered them to keep working and cut the yapping. Some resented him, being seasoned veterans and good soldiers. The rest just did as they were told. Inside of an hour we had everything unloaded and in the fort.

The fort was divided into four rooms. One large room for the PF's, the other for the advisors. One for Sergeant O'Donnell and Corporal Beck, their squad leaders, and the last room was large enough for supplies, ammo, weapons, rations and all their gear. Though the place was primitive looking, the walls were strong and sturdy. O'Donnell, Rich, Quirk and Beck made their way to the NCO room. In the NCO (Non-Commissioned Officers) room there were maps, grid locations, radios and a card table in the center where they talked. Next to each wall was a cot where O'Donnell and Beck slept. All in all the fort was well put together.

After finishing our detail Tucker had the remains of the convoy back on its way to Kiem-Lai II. No one was on foot, so travelling wouldn't be too bad. The rest of us gathered around the front of the fortress as if tourists browsing through a market place. Near their front lookout bunker they had a new starlight scope, powerful binoculars with dials and controls that made it look complicated. The scope was mounted like the one on 335. It gathered its energy, power or reflection from the stars. This made everything in the jungle and paddies visible at night. It gave colors to everything so they stood out and movement was easy to locate and impossible to camouflage. Once you were used to one you felt lost without it. The fortress really needed one. Its position was delicate and although it was well protected and somewhat hidden, it presented an open invitation for any VC in the valley.

Night was starting to creep up. Most of us were making friends with the PF's and feeling comfortable just being around the fortress. Coming to the fortress as we did, helped relax some of the tension and took some of the worries that were mounting. The PF's were funny. They tried to imitate the men in the platoon, telling jokes and practicing their English. They instantly took to Ferrara with his muscular torso and carefree attitude. They were all striking poses like weightlifters or bodybuilders, trying to compare their tiny biceps to Pete's. He laughed and picked them up, two at a time as if weightless. The PF's in the fortress carried carbines, some carried 16's but most carried carbines. Two of the men traded off weapons with the PF's getting the feel of them. Some of the men traded Salem cigarettes for souvenirs. The atmosphere was lighter and relaxed. We needed the change.

Rich came out with Quirk and the rest to brief us. We were staying at Number One for at least two days, hopefully till we teamed up or got flank support from another platoon or even a company of Marines. In the meanwhile we were to run night patrols and watches with the PF's and advisors. During the day it was possible we would make our way into the ville to check activity, gather intelligence and hope to establish some communication. Whether it upset the enemy or not, the Lieuteant didn't care. We weren't sure the enemy cared. At this point the village was hopeless to recover anyway. The possibilities of making them an independent authority free of VC supremacy was beyond repair at least in my mind. The village was either too scared or too brainwashed. No one knew for sure.

As the darkness grew, Rich ordered the first night patrols. I was to lead one, Ferrara another and Quirk the last. A fourth patrol composed mostly of PF's with two advisors were to act in flank support behind us. Soon we would have our finger on the pulse of what we were hoping was not evident.

January 3.
Third Entry.

We've reached *"Number One"* and it's a welcome sight. It resembles the old Spanish Haciendas, like the kind from Tyrone Power's old movies. It has a warmth to it, that makes it feel like home. Rich looks better, so do all the men. Coming here was a good idea. It's a refuge in the storm.

—Franky

CHAPTER 16

"Breaths Of
Silence"

Quirk took four of his men along with one of the
PF's and one of the ARVN's. They headed out first,
acting as point patrol. I followed with Ferrara and
his squad and the PF's were last. Once we were in
sight of the village we' continued the separation.
Quirk left point position and took his patrol across
to the outside of the ville. He covered the area
directly behind Kiem-Lai. We moved to the front
area outside the village. Ferrara was holding back at
least a hundred and fifty yards from the village. Our
position was to hold within thirty yards of the
village. The PF's continued a sweeping motion,
acted as a wedge in the event of a heavy engagement.

Our main purpose was to act as observers and not
killer teams. We already suspected their presence
continuining to build in and around the village but
we needed more specifics and information. We also
had no accurate idea to the numbers involved and
where they predominantly came from. We needed to
avoid a confrontation at all costs mainly because if

their numbers were large, our attack or ambush would be suicide. At the same time it would jeopardize the chances of surveillance and gathering intelligence for battalion. Battalion's concern became more evident, with good reconnaissance we could provide the necessary date for them to annihilate the enemy.

Quirk started to break away, heading east towards the rear of the village. The bush around the village was thick, all the way back to the fort, except for some small strips leading to different trails. We travelled some of the initial trails used by the PF's in the past. Our movement was steady and moderate. Anything of metal, other than our weapons and ammo was left behind to avoid unwanted noises. There was no conversation and no startling movements, only breaths of silence. Our feet never dragged. They were firmly planted with no scraping or dragging motions. We listened, with complete concentration we listened. Though the night was black, we watched. We couldn't keep too great a distance between each other because of the darkness. The man in front of us was God. While observing everything around us, we never lost sight of him.

The ARVN's that went with us were scared. I had one with my patrol. He followed me so close that on several occasions I had to push him back myself. They knew what lurked in the valley and deathly feared the VC. I was afraid that in their fright they would return back to the fort, but knowing KuChi would be waiting, and would beat them to death if they did, relaxed my concern.

Soon we were within distance of the village. Ferrara held his position, digging in with his men just between a group of trees that sandwiched a trench. They had excellent placement and could observe the trail leading to Kiem-Lai. Quirk was completely out of sight, making his way to Kiem-Lai rear. The PF forces which were to follow us, could not be seen or heard. They were excellent night travelers and knew the enemy's tactics and habits.

As we moved further on towards the village we felt totally alone. Every little noise was magnified a thousand times to our ears. We cringed at every sound, imagining intonations that probably weren't there.

The sky above was not filled with stars as it had been some nights before. At different moments I glanced up hoping they would appear, attempting to make a wish. My point man was one of the younger PF's who was oblivious of danger. He kept our expedition brisk but temperate. Time passed slowly and the distance travelled seemed longer than a few hundred yards. Franky made sure he was with my squad, even though he appeared nervous at the thought of being so close to the village at night.

For a moment we thought we heard a sound, so we stopped abruptly, peeking in every direction, expecting any moment a barrage of bullets and explosions, but nothing happened. The air was perfectly still, not a breeze or whisper, even the ground stood still. We delayed for only a minute or two, then the point resumed the march. Soon we could see the shadows of the village, telling us we were in position to dig in. In the night it seemed large and I couldn't judge where it began or ended. Our PF pushed us through the thick tangled underbrush which obstructed our direction west. Every branch was threatening as we closed the gaps and held them to make clear for the person behind.

We came to a small gorge that extended for about eight or nine yards. I looked to my right and saw the mouth of the village through some of the bushes around us. It was no more than twenty five yards away. We lay down in the gorge, propping our weapons and aiming them in the direction of the village. Although we were combat ready, we knew we were to avoid contact unless directly fired upon. Holocheck had the LAW with him, which was strong in any engagement and provided some security but nowhere near what we needed. We supposed Quirk to be at the other end and we knew Ferrara had dug in. We affirmed before leaving that there was to be no radio contact. No situation reports in order to keep our security to a maximum. Each squad had radios for emergencies but we did not plan on using them. We lay waiting.

Time passed at a snail's pace. We looked at each other but never exchanged a word. Every man knew he was to scan for activity in the hopes for discerning the enemy around the ville. Franky was next to me. He had the appearance of a frightened boy. His eyes were wide and bright. It reminded me of that famous saying, "Don't fire till you see the whites of their eyes!" I dared not say anything to Franky or he'd clamp them shut.

The night looked like it would last forever, with no actions or signs of movement. The bushes were still. There were no sounds except the heartbeats of the men around me. There were no shadows about. Nothing! Only our doubts, fears and suspicions.

The village was also motionless and quiet. Not a lantern was lit or a voice heard. In the tranquility of the night air, conversations could travel easily but nothing touched our ears. Then it happened. Shadows emerged from the bushes in front of us. They were no more than a few yards away. The bushes and branches rustled as they walked through them. At first they seemed to be coming towards us, but they veered to the right and in the direction of the ville. It was hard to make out how many there were. They appeared to be only a few shadows. Then, like a falling star, a match or candle from the ville was lit, followed by a lantern. There were two lights gleaming in the night from the village. The shadows got clearer and we saw they were heading directly for the heart of the village.

The PF with us stared intently, he barely whispered, "Beaucoup VC." They continued to emerge from the bushes and eventually made their way to the village. There had to be at least thirty, some carrying supplies. They entered the village and from what we could see, two of them went into one of the hooches. They were probably officers. They came back and brought some of their men back into the hut, along with supplies and what seemed to be weapons. Just as I was squinting and leaning forward to get a better view, the sounds of footsteps echoed just a few feet away. We all tightened up. Everyone took hold of their weapons and aimed. There, directly in front of us, arm's length distance, were the boots and legs of patrolling Cong. My heart beat accelerated and my stomach tightened. The blood in my body came to the surface of my skin. My vision was perfect and I saw them stand frozen, as if sensing our presence. Not a breath was taken. Those few moments were eternity. Not even a whisper of wind brushed through the trees. Then, condemning our own fate, their point man took one step forward...Three more and I would be under his boots. Another step and my finger gently pressed against my trigger. My hand tingled and I was a hair from firing. He started to take another step. This would be his last, but he stopped. His boots turned around. Almost in the opposite direction. By some trick of destiny they carried on their patrol but away from where we lay hiding. They continued to move away as if confident nothing was to be found or just fearful of the unknown.

We all breathed easy for a few moments and we darted looks at each other showing signs of relief. Franky was petrified as if to cut out of stone. I touched his arm trying to break the barrier of fear written all over his face. He turned and appeared to come back to his senses.

We all directed our attention back to the village, watching the shadows of the enemy continue to move within the ville. After dropping off the supplies or weapons, they began to make their way back from whence they came. As quick as the Cong presented themselves, they left. There were no more signs of activities or patrols. The sense of their departure brought relief and anticipation from what the rest of the night would provide.

We waited in the darkness for hours to pass, with no further signs of the enemy. The night passed extremely slow and each man felt weary from the strains and excitement of the night. With dawn approaching we gathered ourselves together and began to drag ourselves back. The black of night lightened, looking at my watch I saw it was just 0500 (5 AM). We wondered if all was fine with the other squads, knowing that through the night, not a shot was fired. Marching back, the jungle seemed safe, even though a few hours ago we felt our lives slipping away. Quirk was nowhere in sight, but soon we could see Ferrara who left us earlier. They spotted us, acknowledged, and continued back to the fort.

CHAPTER 17

Exercise In Futility

Quirk and his men entered the front gate of the fort. They returned using a different route. We were minutes apart and gratefully all in one piece. Quirk headed straight for the front entrance and from the look on his face, was busting with news. The PF's came heading for the entrance too. I ordered everyone to secure and filed in with the other squad leaders. As I entered the fortress I heard Quirk's voice echoing the reports of the night's reconnaissance.

"Lieutenant! They're out there. Lots of them. They were all around us. We could almost touch them."

Everyone wanted to report since we all felt the excitement of the night's encounter. Ferrara was busting to talk while at the same time one of the PF leaders was rattling away in Viet-Namese to his officer. It was chaotic with Rich trying to gather the reports all at once. Finally he spoke in necessity.

"Hold on! One at a time. Quirk, what goes here?"

"Lieutenant. They're out there like flies and that village might as well be their headquarters. They were in and out of there last night. They had supplies and weapons. The sneaky bastards. They're up to something."

"Davenport. Did you see the same thing?" asked Rich.

"Yes Sir Lieutenant. Same as Quirk. They're out there alright. We saw them go into the village, like Quirk said. About thirty of them."

"Try SIXTY! Davenport. They came in from my end too and they had their patrols out checking all the areas around there. It's just luck they didn't step into us," Quirk exclaimed.

"The Sarge is right, Lieutenant. We had the same thing. We spotted Charlie heading into the ville and no sooner did we try to get a good look, than one of their patrols rolled down on us a few feet away. It was eerie...a few steps...and we were all gone." I felt the same as Quirk.

"How about you, Ferrara. You see anything?" Rich was checking with everybody.

"Yes, Sir. Two patrols. About a dozen in each. They made their way past us. Probably about the same time Quirk and Davenport spotted something similar." He looked at each of our faces as he spoke.

"Did anything happen?" asked Rich.

"No, Sir. We held tight like we were told. We were placed pretty good and could have torn into them but it was a good thing we didn't because a few minutes later another patrol came from the other direction and they passed us up too. It was getting hairy out there for a while, then things calmed down." Ferrara's voice was softening.

"O'Donnell, what are your PF's saying?" asked Rich.

"Basically the same thing, sir. They saw two or three patrols. They weren't sure if they were the same ones coming back to their original route or backtracking but they're sure they saw at least two. They kept quiet and held their position in a small cove just east of where the Creek becomes a stream."

"Well sounds like we're sitting on some *TNT*. They really are here and they're getting stronger and stronger." The Lieutenant was shaking his head.

"Sir, it's been like this for days now. We've avoided any contact at night because we know they're out there in big numbers. They don't even seem to bother with us. Oh, occasionally we take incoming or get snipered, but they seem to have more pressing things to get done in that village. We've spotted them going in there more than once," O'Donnel said.

"Have you made any searches of the village?" asked Rich.

"Yes, Sir," he answered.

"Well, did you find anything?"

"No, Sir. Not a thing. They don't like us. They don't want us and we feel the same. At times they're smug as if onto something that's gonna give them what they want. Probably to get rid of us. They're too cagey."

"You mean to tell me all this shit's going on and our battalion and Division does nothing about it," exclaimed Rich.

"Sir, they've been lax. First they tell us to continue reports. Then they tell us to be more exact and substantiate. They tell us, you people are coming to resupply and help our night patrols and reconnaissance. We got so we didn't know where we stood."

"*Son of a bitch!* and they're making us go in such a circle that before you know it, we'll run right up our own ass!...How many do you estimate out there?"

"At least two companies, Lieutenant. At least! And that's from what we see. Only God knows what's out there," answered O'Donnell.

"Get me that radio. I'm gonna shake some cages. I want Regimental Command. I'll be goddamned if we get buried here and they're free to run over this valley. For Christ's sake there's probably a whole regiment camping out there like we suspected. They've got a whole company just in villagers!" He was being sarcastic but serious. He got on the radio to Colonel Foster, our Regimental CO. He could override battalion and get wheels turning. Rich was direct. He pulled no punches. We needed troops fast and artillery set up. We needed air support and open communications. Foster was disturbed but hesitant. He ordered further reconnaissance with more exact grid locations, manpower strength capacity, weapon capacity and on and on. There were endless requests of impossible demands. Rich was screaming back on the radio that conditions were critical and time was of the essence. The order returned. *DO AS TOLD!* and battalion would follow surveillance with Broncos (Reconnaissance planes) and surveillance helicopters. The whole conversation was handled in codes and pass names with eluding phrases that made it so difficult to understand that I was confused.

Rich slammed down the radio, and kicked the table across the room.

"*THOSE FUCKING ASSHOLES ARE GONNA KILL US!* What the fuck do they want. Their names, addresses and next of kin. This isn't maneuvers. This is a goddamn war and a sick one."

"I told you, Lieutenant. I've been stymied," O'Donnell said.

"Well today we're gonna go through that village. We'll go through every hooch and bunker. We'll find out who the hot shots are in that village. Who's got the dope. I wanna know which hooch those supplies were dropped off at. I want some answers and I don't care if I have to make up stories. I'm going to get what we need out here or else we're finished. What do they think we're doing, having fun. Do they think we're paranoid...or are these people...*STUPID?* If I have to, I'll get a "bird" out here and go right to Wheeling. He's running the whole show maybe he can get something done. Everyone else is passing the buck!"

January 4.

Dear Diary,
Returning to the fort is a welcome sight. No one has been killed. The action has been great. Many people have died. Last night I felt the fingers of death around my throat. Sheer luck was our savior. For those few moments I froze. My whole body

remained in shock. I have seen death in too many forms and it is ugly. In the jungle, the villes and out in the paddies. The farmers killed and even the children. Everything is a mockery of civilization.

Now we rest and my whole body feels the weariness of the war. Seeing the light after our watch was the splendor of God or whatever has freedom from this kind of existence. I know the enemy is all around. It's obvious, yet we face them by ourselves. We find them everywhere and there is no escape. Their numbers grow every day. For each one we kill, two more appear, and so on and so on. The whole struggle seems useless. I can't see the point in fighting except to survive. Survival means everything to me now. I must survive to *live!* Survival? I must live to see a better life than this. To find sanity again. I crave for a soft bed and a warm meal, with friends, with good plain clothes. Not to carry a weapon or to fear the night. I yearn for my family and their love. For a girlfriend, for passion to live and love and enjoy life. I long for soft music and walk along the beach, for good books and quiet...the quiet of war.

I want to write more but my thoughts have drifted. I would rather relax and think of them and try to believe that someday all my dreams will come true. Moma always said "you love even the ones that hate you." Dad always said fight like a man. Right now I'm somewhere between the two and I can't understand either.

—D'Amini

CHAPTER 18

Search!

"Quirk, give your men some sack time. Same for you, Davenport and you Ferrara. Later on, I want some men on that village to search those hooches. Poke around and see if you can find anything. You better bring KuChi along with you and some of these PF's. I'm staying here by the "box" and go over some of these maps. O'Donnell and Beck will be with me."

"Sure 'nough, Lieutenant. Anything else?" asked Quirk.

"No, but make sure you and the other squad leaders get some sleep too. I've got a feeling there might not be a lot of sleep time available soon."

The Lieutenant was up tight and with good reason. It was apparent there wasn't enough time to provide headquarters with all the data they considered necessary to make a decision. Time was short and any delays were blessings for Charlie.

It took little time for the men to nod out. They were all exhausted. Eliminating the squads sent out the previous night, there were only half a dozen men from both platoons left to cover the fort, aside from the PF's and advisors. With the casualties taken in both platoons our manpower was low. Many of the men who were on night patrols, would be back in the village in a few hours, searching for some sign of our adversaries. Then they would return only to more patrols at night with more dangers. The men we left behind last night, rotated watches and tightened security in and around the fortress.

I wrote a few lines to Ginny, knowing there might not be opportunities later. With everything serene, my mind was at ease. It was one of the rare moments I could write without showing all the anxieties of war.

January 4.

My Dearest Ginny,

It's 7 AM and most everybody is asleep. We've just returned from our night patrols and secured for the morning. Not a shot was fired by us or the enemy. Maybe all those prayers of yours are working. I don't expect to have any problems today either.

It's such a beautiful and peaceful morning. A perfect time to write and think of you and Jay Jr. I miss the little bugger. Is he growing hair yet? You know...everyday I picture him just as I left him but he's probably growing like crazy. I've shown his pictures to the other men at least a dozen times. You better send me some new ones. They're getting tired of these. The only one who acts genuinely interested is Franky. He's like a younger brother. We've got to have him at our place when we're out of here. Maybe we can introduce him to one of those good looking girlfriends of your (you know with the nice bazoomies). He's a good man. I know they'd like him, so will you.

I hope Mom and Dad are alright and your parents too. I don't get a chance to write my folks as often as I like...and I don't know what to say, except to repeat the same amenities. I don't intend to upset them or get worried. Tell them I'm OK and I'll write again...soon.

Now for the most important part of this letter. How's my lover? You know the one I haven't been sleeping with due to circumstances beyond our control...OH! Listen! I checked with our headquarters again and we should be on for R & R (Rest and Recuperation, Ha! Ha!) to Hawaii in March or April. It seems an eternity but before you know it we'll be together. Believe me love. I'm counting the days, hours and minutes. By the way, first thing I want, when I get off the plane is a lay, or did I mispell that. Should it be lea or lai?...Well you figure it out. I'll take either but I think I prefer my spelling!

Before I get carried away and make love to you scriptuvaly...you gorgeous creature you, I'll compose my passions and save them for more important things like digging toilets.

By the way. If you're interested in a frivolous roll in the hay with me, just blink twice in the next letter and I'll get the message. It'll be our little secret.

I think I'd better sign off. I love you with all my heart. I want to hold you so bad I can't stand it. Take good care of my son. Kiss him for me. Keep him *strong, good* and *loving*.

I am forever yours,
Jay

After a few hours sleep the men were up and around. Quirk ordered everyone ready for the move into the village. In spite of the danger that registered the night before, a handful of the men packed extra rations and supplies to barter with the villagers four souvenirs, grass, sex, or any diversions that provided a release from the depressions of fighting. Quirk made it clear, especially after Rich's orders, we were not making social calls. Our sole intentions were to draw out information, search for enemy supplies and weapons and solidify connecting the villagers with the VC military strategy.

Two of Quirk's men had started an argument over some extra rations and cigarettes. Mullens, a tall, heavy-set Texan with a mean disposition and a poor attitude was swearing at Girard, a smaller man. Girard appeared pleasant but nurtured the same meanness Mullens did. Their argument got louder with Mullens knocking Girard down. Quirk liked Mullens—they were one and the same. He immediately interceded to stop the ruckus, clearly showing his favoritism for Mullens.

Holocheck, one of the senior men in time of the platoon, was telling jokes to the audience of Country, Ferrara, Grayson and Franky.

Holocheck, who also sported a Southern drawl, tried to avoid taking things seriously. He had a strong belly laugh, with the stomach to go with it.

KuChi was briefing the ARVN's. He sounded solemn and stern. He didn't reflect the lightheartedness of the rest of the men. He knew he would play an important part in the breaking down of the village, along with his men.

The rest of the men stashed their gear or stood waiting. One of Quirk's men, Jim Cooney, a New Yorker with a charming appearance and vocabulary to match, was scratching maps in the dirt. He was laying out a picture of where he thought the enemy was positioning their forces. Cooney was intelligent and well liked. He was a former high school teacher and track coach in Long Island. The teacher cut backs and still being single were just the ingredients to push him into the challenge of being an enlisted Marine. He waived the opportunity for Officer Candidate School.

At last Quirk got the word from Rich to move out. Not an ounce of fear visualized as each man took formation, filing out of the fortress gate. The whole atmosphere was surprising when you considered the previous night's events. All the tensions that had been mounting seemed to release with the change in attitude. I, like Rich and O'Donnell didn't like the total change and prior to leaving we tried to impress everyone with the serious problem at hand.

As we advanced through the jungle around us was peaceful. There were no signs of the enemy or any movement that indicated danger. The sky was clear and the sounds of nature give the jungle a park-like atmosphere. Each man was careful though, keeping distance between each other and looking combat ready.

We detoured to a more travelable road, ignoring some of the risks created when openly exposing ourselves. In the distance we heard the hum of a plane's engines. As the sounds got closer we realized it was one of our Broncos (reconnaissance plane), dispatched by battalion to follow up on Rich's allegations to Regiment about the major offensive.

The Bronco flew overhead, traveling directly for Kiem-Lai. It circled the entire area several times, then turned back towards us, creating larger circles of surveillance. The plane was designed to take photographs and layout an entire picture of Kiem-Lai and the land surrounding it. She was thorough in her sweeps, glides and turns. She covered the total area for a radius of at least a mile. Then as quick as she appeared, she disappeared in the clouds, heading back for battalion and what we hoped was a supportive picture of what Rich had asserted.

No shots were heard. For a brief moment some doubts went through our minds as to why the enemy hadn't made some effort to bring her down. The whole matter was puzzling but we continued on, taking no fire or harassment from the enemy.

The village of Kiem-Lai was in sight and the trail leading to her was clear and unweathered. There were older men and women tending some of the small paddies outside the village. As we came closer to the village a few of the older children came running out. They were chattering Viet-Namese and begging souvenirs like the children in Kiem-Lai II. Two of them stared at us as if filled with hate and contempt. The others seemed mindless of enemy sympathies and continued to jabber in Viet-Namese. KuChi as always shooed and shouted them away. Some scattered, others weren't fazed.

Without wasting time, Quirk ordered a search of each hooch and bunker. He dispensed with formal salutations to the villagers and wanted results as soon as we entered the ville. Each man was assigned hooches and areas to search. Under no conditions were we to be persuaded not to search any area. KuChi was to question any of the village leaders and interrogate anyone he suspected in connection with the VC organization in the ville.

The village was busy, with many of the children running free in the streets. Some of the women were carrying babies and some rice. Most of the people were shabbily dressed. There was a small market place in the center of the village where many of the old women and men congregated. There they traded, gossiped and exchanged information about news in the field. Many of the old people had sons serving in the war, unfortunately for North Viet-Nam. There were animals and dogs running loose in the streets. By in large the village was undisturbed by our presence.

Some of the old popasons and momasons nodded as they passed. The rest ignored us. Many of the younger women took refuge in their dwellings avoiding the remarks, glances and advances of the American Marines. The younger women of Viet-Nam were so often of one extreme or the other. They either adhered to strict moral guidelines and never entertained having sexual relations with the soldiers or they accepted a life of prostitution. A few provided total support for their families through prostitution. Generally, these women were looked down on and considered second class citizens. Kiem-Lai had a small percentage of prostitutes and the number had become even smaller with the VC concentration. Some of the women were puppets of the VC intelligence. They provided information from their American lovers of current military activities they were engaged in. They often provided liquor or marijuana along with sex. The libations released what normally was guarded information. Occasionally an American was registered missing in action, when in reality the action they were engaged in was not of the highest military regard.

The hooches in the village were old and shabby. The majority were formed of thatched bamboo and clay. The richer dwellings were made from mortar or cement. These belonged to the more important families or political heads.

I was assigned a small group of hooches at the mouth of the village. The first hooch was larger and more finely constructed. There was a small front yard with a dog and child moving about. My presence was acknowledged immediately as the family elder and his wife stood in front of me asking questions and making remarks in Viet-Namese. I ignored their remarks, not understanding the Viet-Namese. I began to search as ordered.

The inside of the dwelling was simple with a few chairs, an old table and stove. There were some pots and utensils hanging on the walls, and some books lying on the floor next to a beaten hutch or desk. I went through the hutch and books. There was a basket in the corner of the room, filled with rice. I poked through it with my K-bar (bayonet), finding only rice. Near the basket was another opening leading to a room, just as large as the one I entered. The room had cots and bed rolls, enough to sleep five people. There was a picture on the wall of an old Viet-Namese man, most likely a political figure or family head. I turned over the cots and bed rolls and found nothing. There was an old crate in the corner with pipes and tobacco lying on it. I turned over the crate and again found nothing. All during my search the eldest family member, an old, old, popason, followed me making comments he mumbled in Viet-Namese. For all I knew he could be calling me a capitalistic pig. From the bedroom extended an exit which led to a bunker in the rear of the hooch. The bunker was strong and large enough to accommodate a dozen people, packed tightly. The bunker was empty except for a carbine rifle hidden behind some of the sand bags, wedged in the corner. I turned to popason and made a gesture of query with the rifle in my hand. He rattled off Viet-Namese.

I left the hooch and went out on the street. A good deal of the men were not as gentle as I had been.

Several were overturning baskets of rice spilling them over the streets and yards. Some knocked down fences, many were making a mess of the contents in each of the dwellings. I carried out the carbine and called KuChi over. He took the carbine and started yelling at the old man in question as to the reason for the rifle. Apparently the old man was fabricating some story as to the necessity of the weapon. I continued my search of the other hooches, finding nothing. Whatever was left in the ville the night before was hidden so well that the entire platoon met with the same results I did.

Quirk and KuChi gathered the village leaders in the center of the village. They were deeply engrossed in questioning the chiefs. There were men taking advantage of the situation, taking souvenirs that they fancied. The search seemed chaotic with Quirk insensible to what happened.

The platoon was spread clear across the village. The villagers passed from guise of unconcern to expression of worry as many of the marines were callous searching through the hamlet.

Just prior to entering the third hooch I was to search, I saw Mullens, the tall obnoxious Texan, draw his bayonet and cut down water jugs hanging from a hooch. They fell to the ground and broke into pieces. An old woman was cursing him and he shoved her aside. There was a small child about the age of three, hanging on his side trying to pull some of the candy bars, hanging from his pocket. Mullens turned to the child and stabbed his bayonet in the child's right eye. The child shrilled a scream of agony and ran, tripping and clutching his eye. The blood rushed down his small hands. Doc Wesson scurried from across the street, tripping on his own feet in an effort to scoop up the child. The villagers stood horrified, many screamed. Then from out of nowhere I saw Franky leap across the fence, as if he had wings. He landed directly in front of Mullens and with every ounce of strength he could muster, he slammed Mullens across the face, throwing him squarely on his back. Not a second lapsed and he was on top of Mullens with his knees and legs, pinning his shoulders. He was pounding him over and over, totally overtaken with burying his head in the ground. He showed no mercy at all. Country ran from behind and pulled him off. Mullens face was covered with blood. Wesson, two of the PF's and one of the villagers were holding the child while Wesson tried to stop the bleeding. He yelled over to Grayson, who had the radio, to call for a medivac. Grayson wasted no time.

Country was still holding Franky who had calmed somewhat but still bellowed his desire to kill Mullens. Mullens pulled himself to his feet. He covered his face with his hands, half trying to catch blood and half trying to hide his face. Quirk ran over and questioned Country.

"WHAT THE HELL IS GOING ON HERE?"

Country was loud and quick to answer.

"Your man Mullens just stabbed a baby in the eye...You're lucky Franky didn't kill him!"

"Mullens?" Quirk asked in surprise.

"Yea. Mullens!" Country replied.

Just then Mullens was inching his way towards Quirk who showed no feelings about the incident.

"Mullens you stupid son of a bitch! I've got enough problems without you causing more. It's enough having a war with these gooks. We don't need a war in the platoon."

Franky pulled loose of Country and grabbed Quirk.

"Is that all you're gonna do that *SON OF A BITCH!* He's *CRAZY!* If you don't kill him, *I will!*"

Quirk pulled away from Franky and stood in front of Mullens who dwarfed all three men.

"Now. Nobody's gonna kill anybody. Least of all each other. We'll handle this in the proper way. In the meanwhile let's finish what we were sent here to do."

Franky started in rage again. Country jerked him away straining to cool his temper.

"Relax Man. When we get back, Rich will handle him. He doesn't go for this kind of shit any more than we do. You're getting nowhere with Quirk. You know how he feels about Mullens."

"I swear Country. I'll kill that bastard. What does a three year old baby have to know about this *inhumanity!!*"

With Franky's final words he broke down and cried. Some of the villagers were watching, moved, including a young woman, named Y-Nguyen Van Quang...otherwise called *MITI.*

CHAPTER 19

Children Of
Darkness

Tensions and anxieties were rising in the village
from the inquiries, searches and Mullens' cruelty.
Quirk pushed to complete our assignment. The
medivac we called was quick to respond and within
the hour she circled the village, anticipating attacks,
but receiving none. She set down about a hundred
yards outside the village, in a clearing, surrounded
by paddies. Doc Wesson embraced the child firmly.
The baby was unconscious from pain and shock.
Doc had arrested the bleeding to some extent and
wrapped the child in a poncho. He ran with two of
the PF's to meet the medivac.

Country, in an effort to calm Franky, moved him
away from Quirk and Mullens. He took him to
Miti's hooch, at her suggestion. The rest of the
platoon continued the search for nought. KuChi
made no headway with the village chiefs. The attack
on the child made it even more impossible to secure
responses. A few of the men discontinued the search
and were browsing around the market place.

Ferrara made a friend in a small child when he parted with some of his candy and rations. Eventually the parents came along and shuffled the child back into their home, fearing the same atrocity Mullens inflicted. Al's feelings were hurt. He turned to Grayson who also had a generous nature and started a conversation, trying to forget the parent's rejection.

Country succeeded in easing Franky who suddenly noticed the presence of Miti. She was a beautiful woman, with full lips and large teardrop eyes. Her cheekbones were high and her hair was long and ebony in color. It draped over her shoulders and had a lustre like the glistening sparkle of a ruby. She was no more than five feet. Her bodily features were very sexual, with beautiful oval hips and striking olive skin. Her nose was tiny and her chin had a cleft that gave her feminine face strength. She was curious of Franky, who acted so strongly against one of his own people, for the cruelty to the child. She said nothing, only looked emotionally at the feeling face of the man before her.

Miti's hooch was a simple one. Her parents were killed in Saigon a couple of years ago in an artillery attack. She was at school and was spared. Her father's cousin, though poor, took Miti with them when they migrated north to Kiem-Lai after being suspected of VC political connections in Saigon. The strong Diem regime had inspired anti-VC movements that motivated assassinations of major political factions. The Tham family was considered one of the families listed. In fear of their lives, they fled. Miti's adopted father was old and callous. He cared little for her feelings and bartered with soldiers for supplies, money or cigarettes, giving her trade as a prostitute. Soldiers from both armies, often returned, lured by her beauty. Many of the villagers looked down on her and offered her little friendship. Her beauty and misfortune had become a stigma. Once the daughter of a well-to-do family, educated in the best of schools, had become an abused prostitute in a remote village. The few friends she had, knew of her father and misfortune she faced, but their help was insignificant.

For a few moments Franky was lost in her beauty. He was looking for words when Country broke in.

"Looks like we're finishing up, Franky. We'll probably be heading back. I thought it would be better if I brought you in here, away from Quirk, and Mullens. Man, you sure flattened that big bastard." Country laughed looking for a response from Franky. Franky just stared at Miti, completely overwhelmed by her presence.

"Country...who's she?" he said quietly.

"Her name is Miti. She's a prostitute here but she seems nice," he answered.

"A what?" asked Franky.

"Prostitute. Not bad, huh? She lives here with her folks...not much of a hooch? He looked at her then curiously around the hut. The hooch consisted of two small rooms, with a couple of chairs, some bags of rice and like most of the other hoochs, a small old stove. The rooms were separated by hanging beads that separated the living area from their sleeping area and Miti's "working room." The bedroom sloped down a little as if on a hill. In the bedding area were two cots. There was a third cot under a window, with a poncho draped in front of it, where Miti entertained the men her stepfather arranged to bed with her. Near the bed was an exit which led to a small poorly made bunker. Franky was surprised to hear she was a prostitute.

"My God Country. She's so beautiful!" he said.

Country smiled. "Yea, she is but she probably beds down for half the Cong army, especially with looks like that."

"What's the difference? She's beautiful. These people are a victim of circumstances. She's probably as scared as we are." He never took his eyes off her.

"Anything you say, Franky. We better get going. They're probably getting ready to head back." Country pulled his arm.

"Yea. Fine...I...hate to leave her. What a sight, way out here in this wilderness." He was still staring.

With a gentleness that was only Franky's, he walked over to her and thanked her.

"You probably don't understand but beautiful lady, I truly appreciate your hospitality. I hope this war doesn't destroy something as pretty as you."

Without hesitation she spoke back to Franky who was completely caught off balance.

"Thank you for your kind .words...and I do understand English." She spoke clearly and deliberately and looked Franky straight in the eyes. He was shook and stuttered back a reply.

"My...God...you...sh...do speak English."

"Yes and French. I studied both languages in Saigon."

"Country! Can you believe it? Beauty and intelligence. A flower among the weeds." He was amazed.

Country looked worried. "C'mon Franky. Let's get going. Quirk's the type to take off without us. Especially after that incident with Mullens."

"Yea. Alright...Goodbye Miti." He spoke softly and headed for the street.

"Goodbye." Her eyes followed him as he exited.

They left the hut and found Quirk in the center of the ville with everyone together. They gathered two of the village leaders with the intentions of bringing them back to "Number One" for interrogation. They had located a few weapons, some fragmentation explosives, a case of ammunition and some torn maps and documents.

The villagers returned to their normal activity. The only change was the debris left behind after the search and the lamenting cries of the hurt child's mother, who failed to board the "dust off" with her child.

Quirk placed Mullens behind him and kept distance between him and Franky. One of the PFs led the way out of the village and acted as point for the trip back.

Miti stood motionless in front of her hut. She stared at Franky who never took his eyes off her. Soon we were on the trail back and the village was out of sight.

The trip back was as safe as the trip to the village.

We entered the gates and Quirk dragged the two men and the articles found, into the fortress. KuChi followed close behind. Mullens had faded back by the bunkers, avoiding the confrontation with Franky and Lieutenant Rich. He hoped the whole matter would be forgotten; so did Quirk, who immediately reported everything to Rich except the atrocity of Mullens. Franky stormed in.

"QUIRK IF YOU DON'T TELL THE LIEUTENANT ABOUT THAT SON OF A BITCH, *I WILL*"

"What's this all about, Quirk?" The Lieutenant was puzzled.

"Ah...Lieutenant. Nothin earthshatterin..."

"Why you *Son of a Bitch!!!*" Franky lunged at Quirk, but the Lieutenant stopped him.

"What the hell is going on here? Quirk, I want straight answers."

Before he could speak Franky interrupted.

"His pride and joy. MULLENS!! He stabbed some baby in the eye for no reason. The child almost bled to death. He probably lost the eye. We just put him on the medivac; it was pathetic.

"Quirk, is that true?" asked Rich, showing no emotion, but concern.

"Lieutenant that little innocent child was trying to snatch Mullen's weapon. He just overreacted. We're all a little uptight." Quirk treated the matter lightly, trying to justify it. Franky spoke up.

"Quirk you're full of shit. That baby could just about walk and talk, let alone take a weapon from that 300 pounds of whaleshit and fire it too!"

Quirk still spoke in Mullens' defense. "These kids out here are just as bad as the Cong, even worse. They take advantage of our feelings."

"Feelings, you rebel bigot! You haven't got a feeling in your body!" Again Franky jumped ready to lunge for Quirk.

"OK, OK. Hang on D'Amini. We've got enough problems without fighting between each other." Rich stood between the men.

"But, Lieutenant. He's trying to whitewash the whole thing and let that *FUCK, Mullens* get away with anything he wants. Ask Wesson or Country. They saw the whole thing!" Franky pointed towards the two men he mentioned.

"I will and we'll have an investigation of the whole matter and Mullens will hang if you're right. I'll see to that myself! That's not till we get back to battalion. In the meantime headquarters confirmed some of our findings out there. They've got some info from those pictures they took. They spotted a whole company of them digging in north. About two klicks from here. They've also got the names of about half a dozen people in the village who have been supplying the VC with intelligence and tactical strategy. *Three* of the six are *VC OFFICERS!* They want us to pick up the six of them and hold them for questioning when the rest of the troops get here."

Quirk hopped up. "TROOPS? What troops. We're finally getting some help out here?"

"Yes. We've got a whole compnay of Marines coming from the east and a battalion of Army boys from the west. We're also going to get air support and artillery. The intelligence people are getting information that they're planning a major offensive for "TET." Looks like they want the valley. Then they'll make their move out of the valley and into the vestibule that should let them sapper their way into our rear support. They want us to get back there and pick up those six popasons, but not till tomorrow noon, just before we team up with them. They don't want to let on to Charlie that anything's changed. They want things to stay as they are. Which is why they've been dragging feet like they have. They probably know all our moves but hold back on giving us a clear picture of everything.'s

Quirk couldn't hold back. He was full of anger.

"You mean those motherfuckers back there have been using us as guinea pigs? All the while they knew these gooks have been planning to take the valley and were out here alone! *GETTING THE SHIT KICKED OUT OF US,* losing men left and right and playing footsy with these goddamn Charlies!"

"From what I can put together, Quirk. Whatever information they had they couldn't substantiate it, without continuing our sweeps. Allowing the VC to build up, thinking we had no idea of the major offensive."

Quirk was back again. "And allowing them to annihilate us, while they gather data. SHIT!"

"They've been playing a cat and mouse game with each other and I guess we're the cheese." Rich was talking calmly but disappointed.

"How did you get all this dope. I'm sure they didn't spell it out to you over the radio?"

"No. A recon team pulled in while you people were out. They were dropped off when you people called in that "dust off" for the kid. They're backtracking now to Kiem-Lai II to keep some of the people near there on alert. When I started shaking cages and calling Regiment, they got scared I might tip the boat, especially if I started tearing that village apart. Up to now, they just wanted us to keep gathering data, until they made their move."

O'Donnell was quiet all the time Rich spoke, then he pointed a question.

"Then why didn't they brief us originally?"

Rich thought for a second and looked a little aggravated, then he answered.

"That's my bitch, O'Donnell! If this thing was gonna turn into a kamikase or suicide mission we should've known what the hell we were getting into. Look, I believe in taking orders but this might be insanity. It already is and I think they had a good idea of everything a good while back. I feel like telling them to stick this operation up their ass and believe me I'm going to get a hold of some necks when we get back. There's gonna be some reckoning for everybody. Now we just play it their way till tomorrow, otherwise it *will* suicide. Tonight we send out patrols like usual. We play it cool and tomorrow we pick up those six popasons to turn them over to our people. We do it right before the cong get on to everything, then we move them out of there."

Quirk looked intent trying to grasp the scope of the whole plan. Then he lit up as if struck with knowledge. "Lieutenant. We got two old popasons with us. We just picked them up in the ville. What if they're two of the ones we get tomorrow?"

"Shit! We can't let the VC think we're on to them. Get their names and if they jive with what we've got, play it straight. Slap 'em around a little bit. Ask the usual question, nothing that's going to give them an idea we know their game plan. Ask them if they have seen any Cong lately. Ask them what the weapons were for. Try to make it look like we still want to win them over to our side, like we still care about them. They might even be guerrilla officers. You know, make it look good. Then send them back with a squad of PF's or something, so they don't think we're shit scared. But they're probably going to start moving fast, cause they know we're starting to catch on, especially after that Bronco flew around playing candid camera."

Quirk and O'Donnell still looked worried. O'Donnell voiced a question that I think we all had on our minds.

"Lieutenant. Do we really have enough time to hold out till our forces come in?"

Rich looked grave. He hesitated to answer; finally with a solemn voice he did.

"I gotta be honest. I don't know. They're moving pretty fast. Charlie's probably onto as much as we are at this point. Who knows? We just have to hope for the best and that they don't make any moves till late tomorrow. Noon's the earliest our forces will get here. We'll send our people in tomorrow, just before noon, to pick up the six VC and hold them till they get here...If you're into praying...better do it now.

CHAPTER 20

Love And
War

The meeting was over and we were startled at the game plan headquarters had prepared. There was some embitterment because of the deaths incurred the past few days. Everything was cut and dry and with no concern for the individuals involved. We felt inconsequential as we isolated ourselves from one another and took to writing letters or meditating. Now and then you could hear a complaint about the apathy battalion and headquarters displayed in dealing with the enemy without our knowledge or cooperation.

Rich was furious, but composed. He restrained himself in order to avoid communicating dissension among the men. He suspected problems from the start but carried out orders to the fullest. He struggled with his own feelings to overcome them, being aware of the situation and peril they faced, he had to act strongly as the platoon *leader*.

KuChi followed Rich's orders and questioned the village chiefs in a manner no different than his normal questioning. We knew they would not release information, for it guaranteed their death by the VC. They had to believe they were suspected of having touch with the enemy, but they were not to expect we had knowledge of the exact operation. Once the interrogations were completed they were to be sent back to the village.

Franky requested to escort the popasons back to the ville, along with Country, Ferrara, two of the PF's and myself. The Lieutenant was against it but Franky convinced Rich if he returned the villagers along with some supplies, he could make amends with some of the inhabitants, at the same time show our lack of knowledge about the village's involvement. It would also show we feared no major threats in or around the ville. It was a long shot and crazy but it could buy us a little more time, till our entire force joined with us.

I was amazed at the courage Franky began to show but I also wondered if his thoughts weren't really flashing back to Miti. She was the lovely girl he couldn't stop staring at as we left the village and probably the face he had in his mind now. Franky had the look of infatuation then and it could have been the fire that ignited his courage now. While trying to gather the supplies and hasten our return to the village, I couldn't help but look at him questionably, searching for an answer to my suspicions.

We had all the supplies together and were ready to travel. The trip back to Kiem-Lai was quicker than the one a few hours ago. Franky kept the pace swift and brisk, with the young PF leading at point again. There were no signs of the enemy and the jungle presented no immediate threats, as expected, considering the intelligence in the past few hours.

After entering the village we presented the popasons to their families, not mentioning a word or raising a question. Ferrara disbursed some of the rations and other supplies to the children. Franky visited the mother of the wounded child, giving her medical supplies and feed rations. Country traded souvenirs at the market place and I didn't do much of anything, except keep an eye on Franky. It didn't take long to find out my suspicions were right. After visiting with the momason of the hurt baby he headed straight for Miti's. I was tempted to stop him but I thought of our predicament and the perils we faced. I thought of love and hate and war and being a man, and that a few hours' delay wouldn't matter anyway, especially if it might be our last.

Miti was standing in front of her hooch, almost expecting Franky. He made his way to her and when he was directly in front of her, he froze, completely captured by her presence. He stood that way for a couple of minutes then together they walked inside. I envied him myself. Later that evening in a moment of recollection he explicitly shared with me the beauty of that afternoon.

Her hooch was different this time, unlike the conditions that brought him there earlier. This time it didn't seem dirty and old. It wasn't intimidating. The beads leading to her bedroom swayed ever so lightly as if just parted. While standing in the main room, Franky touched her hand gently and affectionately. He brushed her long black hair away from her eyes. Then he looked into her eyes with all the love and feeling a man could convey to a woman. A million years of war couldn't break the bond he made in those few moments. Over the years Miti had grown strong, hard and unfeeling but in those few moments the experiences of her lifetime were behind her. This man was different. He was not cold, uncaring and ruthless. He did not conquer and laugh. He was not an animal, bartering for flesh. He was a man with a mind, a soul and a heart.

She looked away for a moment, trying to escape the uncomfortable feeling that made her a woman but not for long. Franky just held her hand tighter, all the while not moving. She looked back up again and met his eyes. This time they spoke to her and she quivered inside. He picked her up and held her tight, carrying her through the beaded doorway into her bedroom. She felt secure and laid her head against his shoulder. He stood her back up in front of her cot. The poncho was pushed aside and tied against the wall. For seconds they stood there, helpless. She gave a look that seemed maternal and unbuttoned her blouse, never taking her eyes from Franky. Her blouse draped around her shoulders, then fell to the ground. She let her pants fall in almost the same manner. Then she stood before him, naked and beautiful. Her breasts stood firm and inviting. Her tiny waist curved to her hips, that rounded perfectly to her thighs. Her skin was faultless, light olive and glistening.

Franky stood motionless, beholding her elegance. He took one step closer, a breath between them. He touched her shoulders with both hands and pulled her close against him. He pressed his lips to hers, softly at first, to taste their sweetness, then passionately. He leaned her over then laid her gently on the cot, his eyes still fixed on all of her. His clothes fell quickly and he lay next to her. Her breasts were firm, yet soft under touch and he kissed them entirely, not sparing any part of them. Her nipples were hard and erect, full with her own passion. He kissed them ever so lightly, then took each one in his mouth, licking and drawing them in at the same time. His hands were exploring curiously but passionately as they made their way down to Miti's smooth thighs. He was rigid and throbbing and turned to lay on her. She spread her legs enough to allow him entry but close enough to bring his hips back into her. Filled with desire he pushed into her. She was wet, soft and sensitive as she took him. Their lovemaking was rhythmic and exciting. The sweat fell from both their bodies. Their moans and sighs were deep and intense. They met in ecstasy and travelled among the stars, climbing together they touched the zenith. The war around them disappeared. The killing, hate and poverty was gone. The thousands of miles that once separated two entirely different people became meaningless. Their beliefs and frustrations were left behind. Their fears were unimportant. All that was important was their love. The two became one and the one was whole.

Time was becoming scarce and soon Rich would send a squad to find us. I ran to Miti's hutch and hollered for Franky to hurry. We had to head back before dark. There was quiet for a moment, then he shouted back he was coming. I turned away trying to avoid sharing his experience. He kissed her goodbye and wiped away her tears smiling. He told her not to worry. As he turned to leave she called for him in an effort to warn him but within seconds he emerged dragging his carbine rifle and magazines. I smiled for a second and he smiled back. We gathered the rest of the squad and headed back to the fortress.

That evening he sat quietly, writing in his diary and dwelling on his thoughts, before the night's patrol began.

January 4.
Second Entry

Dear Diary,

I find I must write again today, for my heart is bursting with happiness. Today there was no war. For a brief while, I was given reprieve, like a prisoner that was sentenced. What once was bitterness is now compassion and love. The empty walls of my life have been rebuilt with a foundation that will not shake. What once surrounded me and threatened me now has no power...My heart is filled with *MITI*.

All my thoughts are clean now. My vision is clear. The killing still exists but so does love. If enough people find love the war will stop. It cannot go on. Everything and everyone around me are new. I am amazed at the difference.

I will live and survive another day, not to see the war's finish but to bring me another day closer to my life with Miti. Fate has allowed me an escape, a blessing a moment of victory and happiness, a rebirth!

I shared the experience with Jay. I don't want to hide it. I had to tell him. He is my friend and a true person. I want him to see Miti as I see her, as I know her. I will keep her inside me tonight and I will be strong.

—Franky

CHAPTER 21

The Final
Hour

The pendulum of waiting dawdled as we anticipated the start of our night's patrol. The sky's brightness had settled, so had the day's temperament. Everyone appeared to be counting minutes and looking to the heavens, awaiting the darkness that soon would be sending us on patrol. Occasionally my stomach fluttered with the feeling of butterflies as thoughts of an encounter with the unknown rushed into my mind.

Franky's mood was different. He showed no signs of fear or anticipation. He was propped, sitting upright against the fortress wall. He had a letter in hand, probably from Theresa, his sister, who wrote him religiously.

There were already small divisions in the platoon. Those Marines like Mullens pitting ideas and bitterness against some of the more moderate and easygoing individuals. Girard who fought with Mullens only a few hours ago, was now leading his defense with three or four of the other men. They felt he was right in his attack.

Girard, a con man from way back, had a way of swaying a person's thinking, in spite of the logic, facts or morality. He teamed up with Staller and Perry, two quiet but vindictive and dangerous marines who had weathered the war the longest of any platoon member. Perry was of average height and so was Staller. Both men had purple hearts from skirmishes they encountered in the valley. They were both squad leaders from Quirk's platoon. They usually headed killer teams because they liked Charlie's blood. They both had the largest number of confirms in the platoon. They were "Shorttimers," those having less than ninety days in country to serve. They were cocky and often times cruel, like Mullens and Girard.

Their arguments were strong but still lacked the essence of sympathy for a country and people ravaged by the war for so many years. They lumped all Viet-Namese together, saying the enemy was any Viet-Namese and all Viet-Namese.

Country and Ferrara led the argument against the hardened marines and felt sympathetic of the people and their circumstances. They, like most American soldiers and marines, believed in human decency and the right to live peacefully. They were dead against Mullens' actions and refused to accept the defense of it. Country spoke out vigorously, many times calling Mullens an "insensible cow." Just as the argument was heading for fists, Rich emerged from the fort. He ordered everyone together and instructed us of our squad formation and night action.

"Listen up! In exactly thirty minutes I want squad formations ready to move out. I want the same team leaders and the same men in each squad as we had last night. You men know the feel of the country out there and should be able to carry out the same patrol as last time. I don't want any contact or slip ups. Keep your march steady and together. If you see anything, stay put and watch it. Keep your eyes and ears open. Remember if you start any shit out there it's probably the end of us. We can't fight a regiment of gooks. They'll be down on us like vultures...if they're not planning it already. If everything goes according to plans and they will! you should be back here in one piece in the morning. At that time I'll rebrief you and we'll make ready to join our forces. Hopefully we'll be back in our battalion in a short time and I'll buy the beers. Are there any questions?"

"Smiles" Grayson, who very seldom spoke, posed an important question to Rich.

"Sir. What if we have to engage with the enemy?"

"Grayson, I'm going to tell you and everybody again only so I make myself perfectly clear. *YOU AVOID CONTACT AT ALL COSTS!* Otherwise we might not see the morning. It's impossible for our forces to join with us before tomorrow and I don't think we can hold out all day and part of tomorrow against the enemy with its large numbers. If you're attacked or fired upon, you should have good holding positions. Keep them! Don't waste ammunition and don't split up. Return fire only for survival or necessity. Keep your reports coming in.

If you're fired upon out there it's almost definite they've probably moved in on us here too. In that event we can only hope to hold out as long as we can till our people come to help. We can call in artillery but if they're all around us we're hanging ourselves...Are there any more questions?"

Everyone stood quiet, looking at one another. It was obvious. There were no more questions.

Rich waited, looked around, nodded and gave final order.

"Squad leaders get your men together and *MOVE OUT!*"

With quiet respect we gathered up and left the fortress. No words were exchanged between the men. Shaded afternoon had passed and soon became the obscurity of night. Our squad formations were the same as before. Quirk headed the movement with his people acting as point patrol. I followed with Ferrara behind me and the PF's after him. Our placements were the same as before. Our sole purpose was to observe the ville, the area surrounding it and hopefully the enemy.

Everything was the same as before. The trees, bushes, even some of the gaps in the ground. Travelling the same route that was travelled before in an ominous patrol makes you recognize every step. They form impressions you don't forget.

Knowing the enemy was planning a major offensive and understanding Rich's orders that any contact with Charlie was our death ticket made us fear every step. We were overcautious and that was never good, especially in a war like this one. Each move had to be deliberate and without thought. The senses had to be clear and free of threatening anxiety. This had not become the case. Each man shared the fear of the next. Each man felt any second the enemy would pounce upon us. That in a matter of minutes we would be no more.

Each leader became more precise and exact knowing his obligation to the rest of the platoon to insure safety. Quirk was gone and out of sight again. He maneuvered his people safely, ushering them through the bush stretching from the fort to just outside the village. He turned off and took his position directly opposite us on the other side of the village.

Ferrara made his observation post. As before it allowed him and his men access and perception of the trail leading to our position and the village.

The PF's had the toughest job of acting as a roving patrol and backup force in the event of an attack. They were competent people, all perfectly knowledgeable of the entire area and terrain. They knew the enemy's night tactics also. They would act in a sweeping motion, trying to encircle all of us. They were a buffer between the village, our squads and the fort. If they had to lay for the enemy they had an entree to the stream leading to Binh-lai Creek. It could give some refuge and concealment for preventing a fire engagement.

We approached the sloping gorge that had been our station the foregoing night. We handed each weapon with care as we passed them to one another and crawled in the gully. Our point man, the young

PF, pointed to the village, instructing me to keep a careful eye. Franky was next, moving faster and more confidently than last night. He helped me in, then I helped Grayson.

The whole transaction took a few minutes but it seemed like hours. Once in the gully there were muffled sighs of relief as each man held his breath the entire time. We all directed our weapons to the ville. We weren't concerned with the ground around us except for occasional glimpses. Ferrara was behind us acting as our backbone, with the PF's as his. It was important for each man to study every inch of ground in front and to the sides of us. The PF and myself would take watch behind us at different intervals.

So we laid watching, and we waited and waited. Each man was exhausted but their faces displayed their attentiveness. I glanced at my watch. It registered 2305 (11:05 PM). An eternity of time passed in our minds but an infinity was yet to come. Each tree and bush remained motionless. The village was dark and dead. No one spoke. Every so often one man would look at the other, questioning the mood he felt then guided his eyes back to the village and jungle around us. Franky inched his hand over to mine, then gripped it firmly, telling me not to worry, we were in it together. I smiled and pressed back. Then he pulled it away and stared back at the village. There's a comradery in war that's almost brotherly. Every man gets close to the other, knowing his life, his emotional exchanges and sometimes his sanity is dependent of the other person. Such was the case with Franky. He was a friend, a confident, a psychiatrist, a comedian and a man who cared. The touch we kept with reality was the touch we kept with each other.

The moments of waiting became hours and still no sign of the enemy. We lay waiting and watching and nothing happened. The village remained queit and dark. The plant life stood still. It was beginning to become useless expecting Charlie to appear. We wondered if possible if they lay waiting also or if they had disappeared in the night, deciding to move on, hopefully as far away as possible.

I looked at my watch again. This time it said 0230 (2:30 AM). In a few hours it would be light and we would be back in the fort with nothing to report and nothing to confirm. Just as I started believing the enemy would not appear a lantern from within the village was lit. It flickered in the darkness as though it were going to burn out, but then it got stronger. Franky propped his weapon and Holocheck aimed his LAW. Our PF pointed in the direction of a clump of trees which led to the village. We could see the shadows. They filed out in single formation into the village. There seemed no end to them as they poured from the darkness of the jungle into Kiem-Lai. Another lantern glowed...and another, and another. Soon there were dozens of lanterns on the village, alive and burning. Another group of Cong formed from the opposite direction and they too poured some of their men into the village. The numbers became even larger as they congregated in and around the village. A patrol the size of a platoon passed us not ten yards away. They swept around the village, marking off the entire area. They appeared to be communicating with each other and again they moved the supplies into the village. We all looked in astonishment, estimating their numbers to be at least a hundred or more! They seemed lax and confident as though there were no fears or threats to their activity.

Some of the villagers were moving about and voices could be heard. The conversations were loud and relaxed. I wondered if they were planning their moves and if we would ever see the fort again. They were all around and their supplies look great. They appeared to have mortars and their own small artillery. I saw many of them leaving with more supplies, exiting through the brush. There seemed to be some sort of exchange. Maybe food and other supplies for camouflage of weapons, maps, explosives. It was hard to figure, for all we knew it could've been used as a command post and basing for company leaders's meetings. One thing was apparent; they acted as a unit with the village and their visits were regular. There was the possibilty they had friends or family and relatives within the ville. After all, the population of young men in the village was just about nonexistent. We knew their six intelligence people were there though, two we had today at the fort. It was a good possibilty they were already going over an attack on Number One with the two popasons. They would have some information as to the bunker and mortar placings, along with the general makeup and layout. In the short while they were with us they were sure to get an idea of our manpower, fire power and supplies. All essential data for Charlie. I prayed silently that they would not attack until our forces were closer.

They continued their activity for another hour or so. Then as quick as they came they left. The lanterns in the village had flickered out. Everything was as before, quiet, black and frightening.

My watch read 0340 (3:40 AM). In less than two hours we would be heading back. Hopefully meeting Ferrara and everybody else back at the fortress.

We drilled our attention to the village, expecting another visit, but there were no more. The time was 0525. Ferrara was to join us on our trip back at 0530. With some doubts and hesitation I signalled everyone to climb out and start back. Our PF jumped to the front of the squad and led us back. When Ferrara spotted our squad he quickened his own movement to the fortress, feeling secure we were safe and returning.

There were no problems returning. No contact or confrontations. The whole scene was spooky.

The scene at the fortress was a repeat of the night before, each squad leader hurrying back to Rich to make report. The reports sounded similar except the numbers were greater, so was the supplies and the firepower. Quirk claimed to have seen a company with large weapons and mortars as we had seen. Ferrara saw only the tail end of their company's concentration and a small platoon sweep. The PF's observed another small company making camp north of Binh-Lai Creek. There were no more doubts. The enemy was coming in from all directions, their only contact being the villagers, the major source of their intelligence.

Rich accepted the information with attentiveness. He asked only pertinent questions. We outlined on our maps where they were concentrated or pouring from. The PF's gave the grids as to where some of their other forces were making camp. Then Rich ordered all of us to group together with our men and he would give us a final briefing.

Ferrara and I mustered all the men together and Lieutenant Rich stood in the front yard waiting to give us our latest strategy. He handed some maps to O'Donnell and took a breath before he spoke.

"Men, battalion and Regiment are planning their offensive sometime around noon. It's going to be big with at least two companies of Marines and two companies of Army joining us here in the feild assualt. We'll have artillery, tanks and air support and enough total fire power to push back any enemy build up here. It looks like we might have bought enough time to link with our own companies and support their actions against the enemy around the ville. Headquarters wants those six popasons in the village and before the shit hits the fan. It's going to be our job to get them. A good deal of the VC intelligence can be broken down if we get those people and the assualt could be a lot easier, saving more lives. If an attack starts they're sure to disappear. So this is our plan. At 1100 I'll head a force with Sergeant Quirk into the village. The ones mentioned will go with us. PERRY, FERRARA, DAVENPORT, D'AMINI, WESSON, MULLENS, COUNTRY, GIRARD, KUCHI, STALLER, COONEY, GRAYSON and HOLOCHECK. We might bring a few PF's also. Sergeant O'Donnell, his men and the rest of the PF force will remain here along with anyone else who I didn't mention. By 1130 we should be ready to move out of the village along with our prisoners and move south about a kilometer to the point of the Binh-Lai Creek. There we'll ally with our companies. At the same time two companies will be coming from the opposite direction to join O'Donnell and his people. From that point any further action will be under the direction of Colonel Pryor, Regimental Line Officer. By tomorrow I hope to be squeezing asses and drinking beer in Danang and you men will be with me. Are there any questions?"

We were somewhere between happiness and depression. Understanding and disgust. The whole operation was a sandwich and we were the peanut butter. No one knew what to ask so we all just stood there gaping. Rich had his hands on his hips. His last words were relieving but they were said with an absence of levity and only to calm us. There was no doubt time was of the highest priority and a delay of just an hour by our forces, or even a premature attack by the enemy would insure our doom.

The Lieutenant looked at his watch, turned to O'Donnell, then addressed us again.

"It's 0645. You men have a few hours to rest. Take advantage of it. You've got a long day ahead of you.

All those leaving with Quirk and myself will be ready at 1045 and no later. Am I clear?"

There were a few soft "yes sirs" and one or two strong ones. Rich turned around and went back into the fortress with O'Donnell.

We all kicked around, trying to dissect in our own minds what would be important before the move. A few wrote letters, some sacked out right away. I took my boots and socks off, giving my feet a rest. Franky walked over and put his arms around me, looking at my feet.

"Jay. I don't mean to get personal but with feet like those I'd d keep my boots on."

"D'Amini, you shouldn't talk, you've got feet like a squirrel!"

"I know, that's why I keep them hidden. I'm afraid of them and that's why I'm giving you my expert opinion. Now about your face."

"Franky, why couldn't you join the Air Force?" I decided to give it right back to him. He was in a good mood, even with the imminent danger.

"I'm afraid of heights, besides where else could I have so much fun and get paid?"

"Franky, you better get some sleep. I am. We got *some* time ahead of us." I tried to be more serious.

"Yea. I know but I can't sleep. I think I'm too uptight."

"You're always uptight. Is it the VC or Miti?"

"A combination of both, Jay. I'm afraid of not seeing her again or even worse, her getting hurt." He went from a carefree look to total worry.

"*Franky*. Nobody said this thing was easy and

there's no guarantee for anybody, least of all us. Those villagers made their bed and they might have to sleep in it."

"Yea, but damn it, Jay, not her. She's been forced into something she probably wants no part of. I know her. The same with some of those other ignorant people. They don't know any better. They *don't* have any choice. I *don't want to see her hurt!!*"

He was excited and talking loud. It was no good for him or us if he was too involved. I had to slow him down.

"Calm down. Calm down, Franky. Look! There's nothing definite about anybody in that village getting hurt. All our activity is going to be directed outside the village. The gooks aren't even in the village. So will you relax. Once we get the old men our business in the ville is over. Everything is going to work out. We've bought the biggest peice of time so far and it's just a matter of a few more hours. Now get some sleep and leave me alone so I can."

He turned away silently and walked in the direction of his pack and poncho. He lay down and turned over but I couldn't see for sure, if he fell asleep. My eyes were getting heavy and in short order I was asleep.

I was awakened by the shaking of Ferrara who said it was 10:30. We had fifteen minutes to get ready. Everything was a blur and I wanted to drop my head down and go right back to sleep but I knew I couldn't. My feet felt like they were still sleeping so I bent my toes back before putting my socks and boots on. I looked over at Franky and saw he was all ready. It was likely that he didn't even sleep. He had his pen and diary in his shirt pocket with the tip of it sticking out. More than once I told him he might put a hole in his chin with that thing if he ever fell. He looked like he was reminiscing. I looked around at the rest of the platoon. They all looked as bad as me, several still sleeping. Quirk came into our platoon area and started kicking boots and shouting to get up. The men were moving better and in a few minutes we would all be ready.

Rich filed out of the fortress building at exactly 10:45. He grouped us all together, those that he had assigned to go with him. He gave us all the once over, making sure everything was alright. Then he walked over to Mullens and started giving him last orders before leaving. He just stared hard for a few moments before speaking, then he said in a monotone.

"And you. I don't want any problems from you. *You understand?* One hassle....*JUST ONE* and I'll cut your balls out...with this."

Rich's hand eased to the handle of his bayonet that he wore on his utility belt. He left it there and glared at Mullens.

Mullens was taller and bigger than Rich but he stood with the top half of his body bent back, almost at a thirty degree angle. His face was red and scared. His eyes were glued to Rich's hand, then they raised and he softly mumbled..."Yes, Sir."

Rich turned away from Mullens and gave us a few words before leaving.

"We all stay together. When we get into the ville,

Quirk, KuChi and Ferrara will gather our prisoners. We'll all remain in formation in the center of the ville. I want only one squad at each end of the ville. Davenport heads one and Country the other. When we get our prisoners we take off and head for our checkpoint. There'll be no activity in the village other than gathering the prisoners. If any of them are missing *we leave,* taking whatever's left but I don't think any of them will be missing. They should all be there and intact. We get in and out fast and tag up with our people. Remember we can't afford to hang around there. It's a bombshell...OK. Let's get moving!"

Country led the way out with Rich behind him. We all pulled together and followed. Franky was behind me. Country moved fast and it was only a few minutes before we would be in the ville and back out again, home free. Our steps were exact and quick since we knew the route backwards. Every thought imaginable raced through my mind. My heart was thumping faster and I was hoping everything would move as perfectly as Rich announced. We all gazed around us, knowing the jungle was saturated with the Cong, but there was nothing to see, only more jungle and bush. There were no sounds, only our own. There was the haunting sensation of being watched, but no eyes to see.

As we approached the village, Rich saw it for the first time. He stopped our movement and gazed over the hutches and then back to the center of the ville. He also examined the clearing leading to it. Then he gestured Country to push on and into the village.

We entered the village and saw that it was quieter than usual. Little was happening and few people were moving about. I took Franky and Grayson with me and positioned ourselves right at the entrance to the village. Country marched in, then broke off with Holocheck and Cooney to the other end of the hamlet, guarding the other exit. The rest of the platoon stopped in the center of the village as ordered by Rich. Ferrara, Quirk and KuChi addressed two of the popasons, then headed for three different hoochs. Two of the hoochs headed for were the same ones we took prisoners from earlier.

The children in the streets weren't playing. Some ran into their homes, others just stared from their yards. Little by little a few of the villagers came to the front of their hoochs, some just standing in their doorway or by a window. I saw the villagers staring at our platoon in dead silence and it made everyone feel uncomfortable. Miti came to her front door and looked around curiously, as if searching for Franky. He was next to me and I saw the excitment in his eyes. He was gesturing a salutation to her and she finally spotted him. She had fear in her eyes...and tears. She was shaking her head as if warning him. He took a few steps to see clearer, then like a knife cutting through my brain, I heard automatic fire of an AK47 rifle. Everyone hit the ground and looked to the hooch where the fire came from. It was the one Ferrara went into. We were in shock. No one moved. Ferrara stumbled out of the doorway.

Blood was pouring out of his mouth and his eyes were wide and horrified. He was trying to catch his breath, drowning from his own blood. He took a few steps onto the road, extended his shaking hand and fell face down.

The villagers all disappeared, except Miti who still stood at the doorway staring at Franky. He was on one knee looking at her. I pulled him down and heard more of the AK fire coming from the hooch to the center of the ville where the rest of the platoon was. Quirk came running out of one of the hoochs and so did KuChi. They fell behind some cover and returned fire into the hooch that gave fire. Rich and the rest were pinned down as Ak fire came from a hooch on the other side. It looked hopeless until KuChi threw a grenade, leaving just the other exposed. There was enough fire from all of us directed to the one remaining hutch that it finally became silent. Another grenade was thrown and the dwelling just smoked with no sounds at all. Rich ordered a search of both hutchs. They dragged out two bodies from each. A young man, two old and one woman. The two old men were the ones we brought back earlier and probably the two VC officers. Doc Wesson ran to Ferrara who looked finished already.

Everything was silent, then AK fire rang clear again. This time it hit Doc Wesson, who slumped over Ferrara, holding him. Everything was chaos, not knowing where the next bullets were coming from. We saw that they came from a hutch nearer to us. Rich ordered cover and men were scrambling everywhere. Grayson dropped his radio and ran to return fire from a better position. I had Franky next to me and we tried to estimate where to fire as rounds came from another hutch a few yards away. One round passed overhead and the next hit Grayson, who danced about, then fell over dead. Country ran from the other end of the ville to give support fire with the rest of the men, when automatic fire stopped him. He cried "SHIT" then fired his last few rounds before he too dropped. Rich looked horrified and panic stricken. He tried running to Country, being the closest, but was stopped by a barrage of bullets. He fell face down and crawled to Country, still trying to get to him and pull him from the heat of the fire, but as he reached him the bullets riddled both of them. Rich turned on his side, blocking Country, his teeth were tightly pushed together as if defying them to the end, but he finally fell with his arm over Country.

We were all trembling as our last hope of strength lay dead before us. Lieutenant Rich was our spirit and confidence. Country was our conscience. As the tempest of bullets flew, Quirk ordered sweeping attacks from the center of the ville on the three or four hutches that poured out the unending fire. Holocheck came closer a few feet, fell to his knees and knocked out one of the hutches giving the most fire, with his LAW. Perry and Staller were between two other hoochs that gave fire. They both pulled pins and ran, spinning on their backs and tossing the grenades in the windows. The explosions were quick and the shooting stopped.

There was only one hutch left that gave fire and it too had stopped. There was a chance they fled in fear as the other hoochs were being destroyed. All was quiet. There were no more bullets or explosions. There were dead bodies everywhere. Quirk was still cautious. He told everyone to hold. It seemed over. In the distance we heard explosions, like mortars, coming from where the fortress was. Then it got louder and soon we could hear the distant exchange of automatic fire. I grabbed Grayson's radio and called back to O'Donnell and his men. Their reply was panic, terror and hysteria. They were surrounded by the enemy, taking mortars from every direction as well as AK fire and grenades. They didn't know where to turn. Casualties were mounting and soon they would be destroyed. They begged for help and I shuddered at my helplessness. Quirk yelled over to me.

"Davenport! What's going on?"

"It's Number One. They're getting destroyed. Charlie's everywhere! What are we going to do?"

"Radio battalion. ANYBODY! See if our people are close enough! Where the fuck are they!!"

I was just starting to call when from outside the ville I could hear the rifle fire directing at us. Mortars hit at the other end of the ville where Holocheck and Cooney were. Their bodies flew in the air as if weightless as the bombs fell concurrently. They were all around us and the end was near. Quirk stood in the center of the ville, helpless and frustrated. He turned about over and over again in all directions, confused and apprehensive. He looked at Mullens and Girard, then gave his next order as if euphoric.

"MULLENS, GIRARD, PERRY, ALL OF YOU. I WANT EVERY ONE OF THESE FUCKING DINKS DEAD! I MEAN ALL OF THEM! IF WE GO, THEY GO! ALL OF THEM! MOVE IT!"

I couldn't believe my ears and neither could Franky. We looked in disbelief as Mullens and the rest ran into the hoochs and started firing. In the middle of the rage of battle that was exploding all around us the men ran like madmen, determined to follow Quirk's orders. Woman and children, ran from their dwellings, in all directions into the streets, only to be cut down violently by Mullens and the rest. The sight was sickening. Franky stood up and screamed NO! He ran into the village. I jumped to follow him when I felt a jolt in my side. It threw me around and I wheeled into a small gully next to one of the hutches. Blood poured through my shirt and I realized I had been shot from someone outside the village. I lay on my side, touching the blood, not believing it to be real. I held my hand against the spot where the blood came from, straining to stop it. The pain got stronger and with my other hand I tried to pull myself up, enough to see out of the hole I fell into. Franky was running to Quirk, begging him to stop but the killing went on. Quirk pushed him away and ran over to where KuChi was. Franky ran into the hoochs. I heard more fire, then I saw what I believed would happen. Mullens bounced out of the hooch. His face was a pool of blood and Franky's bayonet was sticking in his eye. He kept bouncing as Franky's bullets sliced him apart. Quirk spun around, saw what was happening, and ran to Mullens who was on his back, dead. There was killing and bloodshed all over. The demon of war had taken possession of everything and no one was to be saved.

The radio was a few feet away but I felt helpless and weak. Perry had a few of the villagers cornered by the marketplace. They were frightened and begging. Two of them were small children who were crying and clinging to their mothers. Perry began to fire, showing no mercy, killing each of them. Within seconds Franky came behind Perry. He shot him three times. Twice in the back and once in the heart as he turned to Franky. He fell next to the group of dead villagers with the look of surprise written across his face.

Quirk was confused and scared. He turned trying to find Franky, but Franky was too fast and too smart. He disappeared again. KuChi was at the exit of the village engaged in a fire fight with the VC outside the ville. Girard and Staller were pushing villagers behind one of the large rice bins, preparing to slaughter them. They butted two of the women and one of the old men with their rifles, as they fought desperately to resist. The villagers were helpless, none having weapons, unlike the few that started the attack. As they pushed together, ready to be massacred, Franky jumped around the bin and killed both Girard and Staller before they had a chance to fire.

My vision was blurred and I grew weaker every moment. I wanted to move but I couldn't. From the corner of my eye, I saw Miti run from the place she stood, into the street and toward Franky. Quirk was stalking Franky, like an animal on his prey. She was trying to warn him. At the same moment Miti screamed, Quirk fired at Franky, hitting him in the back and leg. Franky fell and turned to him. Quirk twirled around still aiming his M-16 and fired again, striking her in the breast. The bullet pushed her backwards and she fell straight on her back. Franky stammered, still clutching his weapon. He shrieked, "My GODDD!" Quirk spun around again, surprised to see Franky alive. He aimed to fire but before he could, Franky shot. The bullet was clean into his chest and heart. Quirk sank to his knees. His mouth hung open. Franky fired again, this time to the head and Quirk perished.

I watched for a few more moments, trying to keep conciousness. Franky half walked and stumbled. His body was like rubber. He tripped twice but picked himself up, heading staight for Miti. His shirt was drenched in blood, so was his pants. I could feel every step he took as he hobbled, determined and oblivious. He made it to her body and collapsed on top of it. The explosions all around got louder and the Cong were seconds away. KuChi was dead as the sappers overpowered him, shooting from all directions. Franky appeared dead atop Miti but he lifted his head as he heard the enemy come closer. He wrapped one arm around her chest, just under her shoulders and with the other he forced himself up. He labored with every bit of strength he had, as he started dragging her body to the place where they had made love. He was crawling, walking and crying. The agony was written on his face. He dragged her dead body a few feet, then fell from his own pain and weakness, but he picked her up again and continued to her hooch. He finally made it to her hooch stuggling desperately to the sanctuary with his lover. I smiled to myself knowing that in his own way, Franky succeeded in his last desire. My sight became a complete fog but I could see the sappers running into the streets wildly. They were overturning bodies and shouting in Viet-Namese. Those were my last sights as my hurt and feebleness disappeared and my fear and dread became the solitude of sleep.

CHAPTER 22

Hero's Bequest

If miracles are created there was one created for me. What I thought was my final rest was only a temporary escape. When I finally opened my eyes I saw above me the white uniform of a US Navy nurse. At first I believed it to be a dream but I soon realized I was in a Navy hospital. A refuge thousands of miles away from the killing and fighting. Clean bed and clothes. I tried to sit up but was restrained to lying down. I had been asleep for days and survived the wound. Our forces had overtaken the enemy and scored what they considered a resounding victory, but at what costs? Two entire platoons destroyed, advisory unit and half of a village of innocent people. But even more important the minds, dreams and ambitions of some truly great men. I alone survived to tell a story that had to be written. I was saved by American forces, moments before the enemy completly destroyed all life. The major assualt not only pushed the enemy out of the village, but almost entirely out of the valley. New strongholds were established as well as perimeter securities with maximum protection against another build up. Militarily they were estatic. There was no conscience or remorse, only decorations of valor and sympathetic letters to surviving families.

In the weeks and months that followed, as with all military catastrophes, there was an investigation. But, as with so many other similar action in Viet-Nam, the whole story and facts were clouded with rhetoric, hearsay and misinterpretations of war. The issues were no longer important, nor was the moralilty or apathy of the military brain-machine.

My voice and pleas were only distant chiming bells of so many veterans who were considered harmless and at mental grips with their consciences. I was one of the ones that "Did not see clearly, the whole picture of strategic war." Ha! Did they see clearly the fear on a man's face? "The facts concerning the atrocities were only images of a wounded, frightened marine." Did they try to stop another man's bleeding? "They were suppositions and not necessarily fact. They were accepted pains of a very complex phenomena, too intricate to be dissected emotionally."

Once the case was closed and all the files buried, I was allowed the remnants of a diary willed to me by Franky. The bequest was written on the first page, in his writing and witness by Sergeant Johnson and Country. It read...

THIS DIARY I LEAVE TO JASON DAVENPORT. TO DO WITH AS HE SEES FIT AND WHATEVER PURPOSES HE DEEMS NECES-SARY. HE IS A GOOD FRIEND AND A LOVING INDIVIDUAL AND FOR

THESE REASONS I TRUST IT TO HIS CUSTODY.

The diary was of course not whole, but what remained I will always cherish, particularly his last entry, which even now brings tears to my eyes. It was made that last day, in the hut with Miti's dead body, as he lay waiting for the enemy's final siege. The writing was scribbled and a bit ambiguous...but the words were clear.

January 5.

Dear Diary,

I have little strength left to write. My body aches and so does my soul. I have Miti with me and we are together at last. The enemy is all around and soon he will be here too, but I have no more fear for I am finally at peace. So many have died and for so many worthless reasons. Will man ever learn from his mistakes or will he only continue wasting that which is so vital...LIFE! I want to continue writing because it is so important. I have touched with the Divine now...and it speaks...through my hands...My last thoughts are.......

Franky died January 5,...but his spirit continued to live.

GLOSSARY OF TERMS

In order to allow a more free and flowing book for your reading pleasure I have listed below several definitions and explanations for military terminology, slang and foreign references. I suggest that you read them first to familiarize yourself with their meaning and their application. The word or phrase will usually appear in quotes, such as "crewshead" with the definition being in the Glossary of Terms for your reference.

A, 4's—U.S. fighter jets used in swift and sweeping ground attacks.

AK, 47's—Weapons commonly used by Viet Cong and North Vietnamese soldiers. Chinese automatic rifles.

ARVNS's—South Viet-Namese soldiers. Name given to men from *Army* of the *Republic* of *Viet-Nam*. Pronounced R-Vins.

Bird—Military helicopter or chopper.

Boom-Boom—Viet-Namese slang for intercourse.

Box—Platoon radio.
Broncos—Military Reconnaissance planes.
Bush—Jungle
CO—Commanding officer
Charlie—Name given to Viet-Congs or Guerillas.
Chieu-Hoi—"Open Arms." or "Surrender." in Viet-Namese. Name usually given to surrendered enemy. For a period of time there was a Chieu-Hoi program where prisoners were promised protection and rewards if they cooperated in surrendering and aiding American troops.
Chopper—helicopter
Confirm—word for confirmation of kill, had same implication, as notches did in the old west for a counting of kills.
Corpsman—Platoon medic—field paramed.
Crewshead—Naval term for toilet.
Croch—Marine Corps
Crocodile—slang for kill or anihilate.
D.I.'s—Drill Instructors in Basic Training.
DOA's—Dead on Arrival, bodies.
Doggies—slang for Army soldiers.
Dust-Off—Medivac. Helicopter shuttle for wounded or dead.
Friendlies—those who posed no threats—usually our own forces.
GI—Government Issue—name for servicemen.
Gook—Derogatory word for Viet-Cong or North Viet-Namese soldiers, but in many instances used for any Viet-Namese.
Grunts—Marine Corps infantrymen, jungle sweepers.

Gungy—slang for tough, hard core, dedicated. In some instances used to imply compliment, in others sarcasm.

Head—short for crewshead.

Ho Chi Minh—Famous leader of North Viet-Nam government.

Hooch—Viet-Namese dwellings or huts, usually made of straw, clay bamboo or supply cartons.

Hump or Humping—to march and carry at the same time.

I Corps—pronounced Eye Corps. Area around and north of Danang leading to the DMZ or Demilitarized Zone.

Jarhead—Marine

Joint—Marijuana cigarette

K-Bar—Bayonet, Survival Knife.

L.Z.—Landing Zone for helicopters, usually portable.

LAW—Light Anti-Armor Weapon. A three foot fiberglass tube which ejects a rocket which is effective against bunkers or heavy equipment.

Medivac—Helicopter shuttle for casualties in the field.

Number One—slang for the best.

Number Ten—slang for the worst.

Newbee—new servicemen in Viet-Nam.

OP's—Outposts, guarding stations.

0311—Marine Corps reference number for infantryman.

PF—Popular Forces. Sort of a National guard or police for South Viet-Nam.

P.I.—Paris Island. Basic Training camp for

Marines.

Point—Scout or lead man on patrol.

Semper FI!—Marine slogan for always loyal or dedicated.

Short-timer—Servicemen with less than 90 days left to serve in Nam.

Sit Reps—Situation Reports or Security Checks. A triple beeping on the radio indicating all's clear in the field.

Six—Staff Sergeant in Marine Corps, usually platoon NCO. (Non-Commissioned Officer).

Smoking Lamp—Cigarette break.

Souvenir—to give or take.

Tet—The lunar New Year in Viet-Nam. Time of celebration.

VC—Viet Cong or Guerilla. The enemy.

Wasted—killed. To die.

Weed—Marijuana

The World—reference to home, U.S.A.

NOTE FROM THE AUTHOR

Some time ago, during the U.S. withdrawal from Viet-Nam, I wrote a piece that was immediately published as a feature editorial in some local newspapers. The article dealt with the disinterest and futility of the war. It talked about the pains of war, for everyone concerned, those who fought who were crippled physically, and mentally. The anguish for the families of these men and the apathy of the politics involved.

After writing the editorial, I was contacted by numerous friends, business associates and journalists who suggested I write a book about Viet-Nam.

For years I've wrestled with my thoughts in an effort to decide if the book should be written. I thought about incorporating many of the things I saw, along with the stories told to me. I thought about writing a book that would not only entertain, but that would serve some useful purpose, giving a picture of the way it was and the way it could have been. Finally, the wheels started to turn and *The Weaning of Francesco D'Amini* was conceived.

This is a story unlike many other war stories. It is fiction, but some of the scenes and circumstances are based on fact. A few of the characters are real, but their names were changed to avoid unnecessary confrontations. Any similarities concerning names, places or actions mentioned herein are purely coincidental and not meant to be true ore real in connection with this story.

The book you are holding deals with people more than war. It relates to the agony of war and the pain of men's minds. It presents problems and frustrations, along with remorse and guilt.

The main characters are people we meet everyday, those individuals can be substituted in this story. The only things unpredictable are their actions, because extreme and unusual circumstances create extreme and unusual acts.

It was and is my feeling something more has to be said about Viet-Nam. Something has to be said about the mistakes, but something also has to be said about the poor courageous souls who gave and gave. If one can experience the agony and fear of war, it should stand to reason that the chances of jumping into another would be slim, but this is one of humanity's greatest disappointments. We speak out enough to make conversation and impress our contemporaries, but not enough to change things.

I hope this book might, in some small way, alter things. While reading this story, I hope to bring you closer to the lives and hardships of the men and women involved. I hope that you can identify with their experience, their victories and defeats. I hope you can become a part of Hotel's platoon and like Franky, log memories in your mind that you never forget.

In closing, I would like to quote my own words from the editorial I mentioned earlier. "War is always a monster and the political masterminds who regulate and control it with current budget reviews, international compromise and voters' priorities, have ignored the very essence of life, that is, the right to use it, in the best possible way and for the best possible reasons.

"They have, as so many times before in history, turned their backs on their brothers and sisters, they claim to love. We are just as guilty here, in our own backyards. We take sides because of the social mores and we try to avoid involvement, involvement with our own boys when they were there and involvement with a desperate country and people. I am not saying there should be more bloodshed and I know only too wel that it is spent uselessly, but what did it all mean? What will it mean?

"Do we have any answers?"

"What will we tell our children?"

"Will it be another part of history that might repeat itself again and again, maybe twenty years from now?

"I pray my children will be spared."

Dominic N. Certo

THE UNTOLD STORY OF

DOUGLAS MacARTHUR

BY FRAZIER HUNT

The definitive story of one of the most
controversial military men of all times,
told by a reporter with a background
of information and experience
that better fitted him than any other to
tell the intimate MacArthur story.

$2.50 ★ #25101

HOUR OF REDEMPTION:

It was towards the end of the War that General Douglas MacArthur organized a top secret commando raid to rescue the five hundred POW's being held by the Japanese on the main Philippine island of Luzon. Many vets claim that this was MacArthur's most daring and strategically executed mission. In this authentic account written by a military expert and verified by dozens of witnesses and survivors, the entire sequence of events surrounding the liberating army's amazing attack has been recorded.

$2.50 ★ 25000

THE RED BRIGADES

JOHN CASERTA

Who are the Red Brigades? What exactly is their goal? This volume by a first-hand observer, traces the beginning of the Red Brigades from their campus origins and shows how they have managed to mount a campaign of terror that threatens the very foundations of Western democracy.

19196 ★ $1.95

SQUADRON AIRBORN

ELLESTON TREVOR

THE GLASSHOUSE GANG
DESERT
MARAUDERS

GORDON LANDSBOROUGH

In which the
Glasshouse Gang continues
to settle their account
with the screws
at Sharafim Prison.
This continues
the story of a
unique collection of
scoundrels whose exploits set
the Western Desert afire.
#15261 ★ $1.50

BY JOHN L. STIPP

A
DOCUMENTARY
OF
NAZI AGGRESSION
1937 (GERMANY)-1977 (U.S. NAZI CELLS)
#19153 ★ $1.95